Rule #1:

You may bring only what fits in your backpack. Don't try to fake it with a purse or a carry-on.

Rule #2:

You may not bring guidebooks, phrase books, or any kind of foreign language aid. *And no journals.*

Rule #3:

You cannot bring extra money or credit/debit cards, traveler's checks, etc. I'll take care of all of that.

Rule #4:

No electronic crutches. This means no laptop, no cell phone, no music, and no camera. You can't call home or communicate with people in the U.S. by Internet or telephone. Postcards and letters are acceptable and encouraged.

That's all you need to know for now. See you at 4th Noodle.

13 Little Blue Envelopes

maureen johnson

HarperTempest

An Imprint of HarperCollins*Publishers*

HarperTempest is an imprint of HarperCollins Publishers.

ALLOYENTERTAINMENT   Produced by Alloy Entertainment
151 West 26th Street, New York, NY 10001

Library of Congress Cataloging-in-Publication Data
Johnson, Maureen
    13 little blue envelopes / Maureen Johnson.—1st ed.
      p.   cm.
    Summary: When seventeen-year-old Ginny receives a packet of mysterious
envelopes from her favorite aunt, she leaves New Jersey to criss-cross Europe on a
sort of scavenger hunt that transforms her life.
    ISBN-10: 0-06-054143-1 — ISBN-13: 978-0-06-054143-9
    [1. Voyages and travels—Fiction.   2. Letters—Fiction.   3. Aunts—Fiction.
4. Artists—Fiction.   5. Grief—Fiction.   6. Europe—Fiction.]   I. Title:
Thirteen little blue envelopes.   II. Title.
PZ7.J634145Aaf 2005   2005002658
[Fic]—dc22

Typography by Christopher Grassi
◆
First Harper Tempest edition, 2006

For Kate Schafer,
the greatest traveling companion
in the world, and a woman
who is not afraid to admit
that she occasionally can't
remember where she lives.

Acknowledgments

I would like to thank the trustees of Hawthornden Castle. This book began there, during my residency, when I also learned to navigate the roads of Midlothian, Scotland, in the pitch dark, in the rain, in winter. (An accomplishment, but not something I recommend.)

Simon Cole and Victoria Newlyn provided safe haven in London and never once asked annoying questions like, "What are you doing here?" or "When are you leaving?" Stacey Parr served as resident expatriate and lovable mad aunt, and Alexander Newman as the Englishman in New York and ever-supportive uncle. John Jannotti is long overdue thanks for sharing his much-varied expertise and for his tolerance of my coffee-drinking.

Without the editorial guidance of Ben Schrank, Lynn Weingarten, and Claudia Gabel of Alloy Entertainment, and Abby McAden of HarperCollins, I would be nowhere at all.

13 Little Blue Envelopes

#1

Dear Ginger,

I have never been a great follower of rules. You know that. So it's going to seem a little odd that this letter is full of rules I've written and that I need you to follow.

"Rules to what?" you have to be asking yourself. You always did ask good questions.

Remember how we used to play the "today I live in" game when you were little and used to come visit me in New York? (I think I liked "I live in Russia" best. We always played that one in winter. We'd go to see the Russian art collection at the Met, stomp through the snow in Central Park, then go to that little Russian restaurant in the Village that had those really good pickles and that weird hairless poodle who sat in the window and barked at cabs.)

I'd like to play that game one more time--except now we're going to be a little more literal. Today's game is "I live in London." Notice that I have included $1,000 in cash in this envelope. This is for a passport, a one-way ticket from New York to London, and a backpack. (Keep a few bucks for a cab to the airport.)

Upon booking the ticket, packing the

backpack, and hugging everyone good-bye, I want
you to go to New York City. Specifically, I want
you to go to 4th Noodle, the Chinese restaurant
under my old apartment. Something is waiting
there for you. Go to the airport right from
there.

You will be gone for several weeks, and you
will be traveling in foreign lands. These are the
aforementioned rules that will guide your
travels:

Rule #1: You may bring only what fits in
your backpack. Don't try to fake it out with
a purse or a carry-on.

Rule #2: You may not bring guidebooks,
phrase books, or any kind of foreign
language aid. And no journals.

Rule #3: You cannot bring extra money or
credit/debit cards, traveler's checks, etc.
I'll take care of all that.

Rule #4: No electronic crutches. This means
no laptop, no cell phone, no music, and no
camera. You can't call home or communicate

with people in the U.S. by Internet or
telephone. Postcards and letters are
acceptable and encouraged.

    That's all you need to know for now. See you at
4th Noodle.

                        Love,
                        YOUR RUNAWAY AUNT

A Package Like a Dumpling

As a rule, Ginny Blackstone tried to go unnoticed—something that was more or less impossible with thirty pounds (she'd weighed it) of purple-and-green backpack hanging from her back. She didn't want to think about all the people she'd bumped into while she'd been carrying it. This thing was not made for wearing around New York City. Well, *anywhere*, really . . . but especially the East Village of New York City on a balmy June afternoon.

And a chunk of her hair was caught under the strap on her right shoulder, so her head was also being pulled down a little. That didn't help.

It had been over two years since Ginny had last been to the 4th Noodle Penthouse. (Or "that place above the grease factory," as Ginny's parents preferred to refer to it. It wasn't entirely unfair. 4th Noodle was pretty greasy. But it was the good kind of greasy, and they had the best dumplings in the world.)

Her mental map had faded a bit in the last two years, but 4th Noodle's name also contained its address. It was on 4th Street and Avenue A. The alphabet avenues were east of the numbers, deeper into the super-trendy East Village—where people smoked and wore latex and never shuffled down the street with bags the size of mailboxes strapped to their backs.

She could just see it now . . . the unassuming noodle shop next to Pavlova's Tarot (with the humming purple neon sign), just across the street from the pizza place with the giant mural of a rat on the side.

There was a tiny tinkle of a chime and a sharp blast of air-conditioning as Ginny opened the door. Standing behind the counter was a pixie of a woman manning three phones at once. This was Alice, the owner, and Aunt Peg's favorite neighbor. She smiled broadly when she saw Ginny and held up a finger, indicating that she should wait.

"Ginny," Alice said, hanging up two of the phones and setting down the third. "Package. Peg."

She disappeared through a bamboo curtain that covered a door into the back. Alice was Chinese, but she spoke perfect English (Aunt Peg had told her so). But because she always had to get right to the point (4th Noodle did a brisk business), she spoke in halting single words.

Nothing had changed since the last time Ginny had been here. She looked up at the illuminated pictures of Chinese food, the shiny plastic visions of sesame shrimp and chicken and broccoli. They glowed, not quite tantalizingly, more radioactively. The chicken pieces were a little too glossy and orange. The sesame seeds too white and too large. The broccoli was so green it seemed to vibrate. There was the blown-up and framed picture of Rudy Giuliani standing with a glowing Alice, taken when he had shown up one day.

It was the smell, though, that was most familiar. The heavy, fatty smell of sizzling beef and pork and peppers and the sweetish odor of vats of steaming rice. This was the scent that seeped through Aunt Peg's floor and perfumed her. It rang such a chord in Ginny's memory that she almost swung her head around to see if Aunt Peg was standing there behind her.

But, of course, she couldn't be.

"Here," Alice said, emerging from the beaded curtain with a brown paper package in her hand. "For Ginny."

The package—an overstuffed padded brown envelope—was indeed addressed to her, Virginia Blackstone, care of Alice at 4th Noodle, New York City. It was postmarked from London and had the faintest aura of grease.

"Thanks," Ginny said, accepting the package as gracefully as she could, given that she couldn't lean over without falling face-first onto the counter.

"Say hi to Peg for me," Alice said, picking up the phone and launching straight into an order.

"Right . . ." Ginny nodded. "Um, sure."

Once she was out on the street, scanning Avenue A nervously for the cab she was going to have to hail for herself, Ginny wondered if she should have told Alice what had happened. But she was soon distracted by the sheer terror that her task caused her. Cabs were yellow beasts that sped through New York, whisking people who had to *be* places to the places they had to be and leaving terrified pedestrians scrambling for cover.

No, she thought, raising a timid hand as far as she could as a herd of her prey suddenly appeared. There was no reason to tell Alice what had happened. She barely believed it herself. And besides, she had to go.

The Adventures of Aunt Peg

When Aunt Peg was Ginny's age (seventeen), she ran away from her home in New Jersey, just two weeks before she was supposed to go off to Mount Holyoke on a full scholarship. She reappeared a week later and seemed surprised by the fact that people were upset with her. She needed to think about what she wanted to accomplish in school, she explained, so she'd gone off to Maine and met some people who built hand-crafted fishing boats. Also, she wasn't going to school now, she informed everyone. She was going to take a year off and work. And she did. She gave up her scholarship and spent the next year waitressing at a big seafood restaurant in downtown Philadelphia and living with three other people in a small South Street apartment.

The next year, Aunt Peg went to a tiny college in Vermont where nobody got any grades and where she majored in painting. Ginny's mom, Aunt Peg's older sister, had a pretty clear vision of what "real" college majors included, and this was not one of them. To her, majoring in painting was an act of insanity akin to majoring in photocopying or reheating leftovers. Ginny's mom was born practical. She lived in a nice house and she had a little baby (Ginny). She encouraged her younger sister to become an accountant, like herself. Aunt Peg replied in a note that said she had picked up a minor in performance art.

As soon as she graduated, Aunt Peg went off to New York and moved into the 4th Noodle Penthouse, and there she remained. That was about the only constant in her life. Her job changed constantly. She was a manager at a major art supply store until she accidentally hit the zero one too many times on an online order form. Instead of the twenty non-returnable, custom-made Italian easels she was supposed to get, she was surprised to take delivery of two hundred. She answered phones as a temp at Trump headquarters until she happened to take a call from Donald himself. She thought it was one of her actor friends pretending to be Donald Trump—so she immediately launched into a tirade on "scumbag capitalists with bad toupees." She enjoyed recounting the experience of being escorted out of the building by two security guards. To Aunt Peg, these jobs were just the things she did until her art career took off.

Again, this caused Ginny's mother to despair over her little sister—and she always tried to remind Ginny that though she should love her aunt, she shouldn't try to *be* like her. There was never really any danger of this. Ginny was just too well behaved, too normal for that ever to be an issue. Still, she loved her visits to Aunt Peg's. Though they were erratic and all too infrequent, they were also magical experiences during which all normal rules of living were cast aside. Dinner didn't have to be balanced and on the table at six—it could be Afghan kebabs and black sesame ice cream at midnight. Evenings weren't spent in front of the TV. Sometimes they wandered through costume shops and boutiques, trying on the most expensive and outrageous things they could find—things Ginny would have been mortally embarrassed to put on around anyone else, and frequently things so pricey that she felt like she needed permission touch them. ("It's a store," Aunt Peg would say as she put on the five-hundred-dollar, saucer-sized sunglasses or the huge feathered hat. "The stuff is here to try on.")

The best part about Aunt Peg was that when Ginny was around her, she felt more interesting. She wasn't quiet and dutiful. She was louder. Aunt Peg made her different. And the promise had always been that Aunt Peg would be there—throughout high school, throughout college—to guide Ginny. "That's when you'll need me," Aunt Peg always said.

One day, in November of Ginny's sophomore year, Aunt Peg's phone stopped working. Ginny's mom sighed and figured the bill hadn't been paid. So she and Ginny got in the car to drive up to New York to see what was going on. The apartment above 4th Noodle was vacant. The super told them that Aunt Peg had moved out several days before, leaving no forwarding address. There was a little note, though, stuck under the welcome mat. It read: *Something I just have to do. Be in touch soon.*

At first, no one was too concerned. It was assumed that this was just another Aunt Peg escapade. A month went by. Then two. Then the spring semester was over. Then it was summer. Aunt Peg was simply gone. Then came a few postcards, basic assurances that she was doing well. They were postmarked from a variety of places—England, France, Italy—but they contained no explanations.

So Aunt Peg was exactly the kind of person who would send her to England alone, with a package from a Chinese restaurant. That wasn't so odd.

The odd part was that Aunt Peg had been dead for three months.

That last fact was a little hard to swallow. Aunt Peg was the most lively person Ginny had ever known. She was also only thirty-five years old. That number was stuck in Ginny's head because her mother kept repeating it over and over. Only thirty-five. Lively thirty-five-year-olds weren't supposed to die. But Aunt Peg had. The phone call had come from a doctor in England explaining that Aunt Peg had developed cancer—that it had come quickly, that everything had been tried but nothing could be done.

The news . . . the illness . . . it was all very distant to Ginny. Somehow, she'd never really believed it. Aunt Peg was still out there somewhere in her mind. And Ginny was somehow speeding toward her in this plane. Only Aunt Peg could make something like this happen. Not that Ginny hadn't had to do her part. First, she'd had to convince herself that she could follow what seemed like an obvious flight of insanity from an aunt who wasn't known for her reliability. Once she'd done that, she had to convince her parents of the same thing. Major international treaties had been negotiated in less time.

But now she was here. No going back now.

The plane was cold. Very cold. The lights were down, and it was completely black outside the small windows. Everyone but Ginny seemed to be asleep, including the people to either side of her. She couldn't move without waking them up. Ginny wrapped herself in the tiny and ineffectual airline blanket and clutched the package to her chest. She hadn't been able to bring herself to open it yet. Instead, she'd spent most of the night looking out of her darkened airplane window at a long shadow and several blinking lights, at first thinking she was looking at the coast of New Jersey and then maybe Iceland or Ireland. It wasn't until the dawn, when they were just about to land, that she saw that the whole time she'd been looking at the wing.

Below them, through a cottony veil of clouds, was a patchwork of green squares. Land. This plane was actually going to *land*, and they were going to make her *get out*. In a *foreign country*. Ginny had never been anywhere more exotic than Florida, and nowhere by herself.

She pried the package from her own grip and set it on her lap. The time had clearly come to open it. Time to find out what Aunt Peg had planned for her.

She pulled open the seal and reached inside.

The package contained a collection of envelopes much like the first. They were all blue. They were made of heavy paper. Good quality. The kind from one of those boutique paper stores. The front of each envelope was either illustrated in pen and ink or watercolor, and they were bundled together with an overstretched rubber band that had been doubled around them.

More importantly, they were each marked with a number, starting with two and running to thirteen. Envelope #2 had an illustration of a bottle, with a label that read OPEN ME ON THE PLANE.

So she did.

#2

Dear Ginger,

How was 4th Noodle? It's been a while, huh? I hope you had some ginger dumplings for me.

I'm well aware that I owe you an explanation about a lot of things, Gin. But let me start by telling you about my life in New York, before I left, two years ago.

I guess you know that I caught a lot of flak from your mom (because she cares for her wayward little sister) for never having a "real job," and not being married, and not having kids and a house and a dog. But I was okay with that. I thought I was doing things right and other people were doing them wrong.

One November day, though, I was riding on the subway up to my new temp job. That blind guy with the accordion who rides the 6 train was playing the Godfather theme song right in my ear, just like he did every other time in my life I've ever taken the 6. And then I got off at 33rd Street and bought myself a cup of burned, stale coffee from the closest deli for 89 cents, just like I did every other time I went for a temp job.

That day I was going to a job in an office in the Empire State Building. I have to confess,

Gin . . . I get a little romantic about the old Empire State. Just looking at it makes me want to play some Frank Sinatra tunes and sway a little. I have a crush on a building. I'd been in there several times but never to work. I always knew there were offices in there, but that fact never penetrated, really. You don't work in the Empire State Building. You propose in the Empire State Building. You sneak a flask up there and raise a toast to the whole city of New York.

And as I walked up to it and realized that I was about to enter that beautiful building to file or make copies--I stopped. Too quickly, actually. The guy behind me walked right into me.

Something had seriously gone wrong if I was going into the Empire State for that.

That was how it all started, Gin. It was right there on the 33rd Street sidewalk. I never went to work that day. I turned around, got back on the 6, and went home. As much as I loved my apartment, something in me was saying . . . it's time! Time to go! Like that rabbit in <u>Alice</u> <u>in</u> <u>Wonderland</u> who runs past saying, "I'm late!"

Late for what, I couldn't really tell you. But this feeling was so intense, I couldn't shake it. I called in sick. I wandered around my apartment in circles. Something wasn't right about what I was doing. I'd been comfortable in my apartment for too long. I was doing boring jobs.

I thought about all the artists I'd admired. What did they do? Where did they live? Well, for the most part, they lived in Europe.

What if I just went to Europe? Right then? The people I admired had sometimes starved and scraped their way along, but it had helped them create. I wanted to create.

By that night, I had purchased my ticket to London. I borrowed $500 from a friend to do it. I gave myself three days to get everything settled. I picked up the phone to call you a few times, but I didn't know what to say. Where I was going . . . why . . . I had no answers. And I didn't know how long I'd be gone.

This is the position you are in right now. You are about to go to England with no idea of what's in store for you. Your path, your instructions, are in these envelopes. Here's the catch: You may only open them one at a time and only once you've completed the task in each letter. I am relying on your honesty--you could open them all now, and I'd certainly never know. But I'm serious, Gin. It won't work unless you open them exactly as I've said.

On landing, your first task is to get from the airport to where you'll be staying. To do this, you'll need to take the underground, otherwise known as the tube (in American, the subway). I've enclosed a £10 note for this. It's the purple thing with the queen on it.

You need to get to the stop called Angel, which is on the Northern Line. You'll be in a part of London called Islington. When you get out, you'll be on Essex Road. Go right. Walk for about a minute until you reach Pennington Street. Hang left and look for 54a.

Knock. Wait for someone to open door. Rinse and repeat as necessary until door opens.

Love,
Your Runaway Aunt

P.S.

You will notice that an ATM card for Barclays Bank is also in this envelope. Of course, it wouldn't be safe to write the PIN number down. When you get to 54a, ask the person who lives there, "What did you sell to the queen?" The answer to that question is the PIN. When you've solved that, you may open #3.

54a Pennington Street, London

She was standing somewhere in Heathrow Airport. She'd been shuffled off the plane, had pulled the notorious backpack from the luggage carousel, waited in an hour-long line to get her passport stamped, and been ignored by some customs officers. Now she was staring at a London tube map.

It looked like a nursery school poster designed to attract the eyes of toddlers. It was stark white, with bright primary-colored lines snaking around it. The stops had solid-sounding names, like Old Street and London Bridge. Royal sounding: Earl's Court, Queensway, Knightsbridge. Entertaining: Elephant & Castle, Oxford Circus, Marylebone. And there were names she recognized: Victoria Station, Paddington (where the bear lived), Waterloo. And there was Angel. To get there, she'd have to change at a place called Kings Cross.

She pulled out her £10 note, found a ticket machine, and followed the instructions. She walked up to one of the entrance aisles and faced a pair of metal doors, almost like saloon doors. She looked around, unsure of what to do next. She tried to push the gate gently, but nothing happened. Then she saw a woman next to her put her ticket into a slot on the little metal box next to her, and the doors opened. Ginny did the same. The machine sucked in the ticket with a satisfying swoosh, and the doors clapped open and she passed through.

Everyone was moving in the same direction, so she kept going, trying not to stumble against the backs of the bags other people were wheeling. When the train slid up to the stark white platform, she didn't think to unhook herself from the pack, so when she got on, she could only fit on the very edge of a seat.

It wasn't like the subway she had taken in New York. These were much nicer. The doors made pleasant bonging noises as they opened, and a British voice warned her to "mind the gap."

The train moved aboveground. They were riding along behind houses. Then it was back underground, where the stations became more crowded. All kinds of people shuffled on and off, some with maps and backpacks, others with folded newspapers or books and blank expressions.

The cooing British voice said, "Angel," a few stops later. She couldn't turn around, so she had to back off the train, feeling for the space with her foot. A sign suspended from the ceiling said WAY OUT. As she approached the exit, there was another set of metal gates. This time, Ginny was certain that they would yield when she approached, kind of like an automatic door. But they didn't. Not even when she walked right into them.

An annoyed British voice from behind her said, "You have to put in your ticket, love."

She turned to face a man in a navy blue uniform and a bright orange work vest.

"I don't have it," she said. "I put the ticket in the machine. It took it."

"You're supposed to take it back," he said with a sigh. "It comes back out."

He went over to one of the metal boxes and touched some unseen button or lever. The gates clapped open for her. She hurried through, too embarrassed to even look back.

The first thing that hit her was the smell of a recent rain. The sidewalk was still wet and was fairly thick with people who politely moved around her and her backpack. The street was jammed full of real London traffic, just like in the pictures. The cars were tightly packed together, all going in the wrong direction. An actual red double-decker bus lumbered along.

As soon as she turned off the main road, everything became much quieter. She found herself on a narrow street with a zigzagging line that cut down the middle. The houses were all chalk white and were nearly identical except for the colors of their doors (mostly black, but occasionally there was a red or a blue) and they all had multiple chimney pots poking out of the top, along with antennas and satellite dishes. The effect was weird—it was like a space station had crashed into a Charles Dickens story.

Number 54a had a jagged crack running down the six concrete steps that led to its front door. Several large pots lined these steps, each containing plants that didn't exactly look like they had been condemned to death on purpose. They were weak and small but still making an effort. Someone had obviously tried, and failed, to keep them alive.

Ginny paused at the base of the steps. This had a very good chance of being a major mistake. Aunt Peg had some very unusual friends. Like the performance artist roommate—the one who ate her own hair onstage. Or the guy who spent a month communicating only through interpretive dance as a form of protest (against what, no one really knew).

No. She had come this far. She wasn't going to give up on the very first step. She walked up the stairs and knocked at the door.

"Hang on a moment," a voice called from inside. "Just a moment."

The voice was British (which really shouldn't have surprised her but still did). It was also male. Not an old voice. She heard a thumping—someone running downstairs. And then the door swung open.

The man standing in front of her was in the process of getting dressed. The first thing that surprised Ginny was that he was wearing half a black suit (the pants). A silver gray tie hung loosely around his neck, and his shirt was only half tucked in. Aunt Peg's friends did not usually wear suits (or even parts of suits) and ties. It was less of a surprise that he was handsome— tall, with very dark, slightly curly hair and highly arched eyebrows. Aunt Peg attracted people with lots of personality, lots of charm.

The man gaped at her for a moment, then hurriedly tucked in his shirt.

"Are you Virginia?" he asked.

"Yeah," Ginny said. The *yeah* came out too broad, and she suddenly heard her own accent. "I mean, yes. That's me. I'm Ginny. How did you know?"

"Just a guess," he said, his eyes lingering over her bag. "I'm Richard."

"I'm Ginny," she said again. She gave her head a quick snap to try to get the blood flowing up there again.

Richard clearly had a moment of confusion over what kind of greeting to give her. He finally stuck out his hand for her bag.

"It's a good thing you caught me. I wasn't sure when you were coming. I wasn't even sure *if* you were coming."

"Well, I'm here," she said.

They nodded at each other for a moment in acknowledgment of this fact until Richard seemed to be physically struck by a thought.

"You should come in," he said.

He opened the door wider and grimaced only slightly as he relieved Ginny of the groaning purple-and-green backpack.

Richard gave her a quick tour that revealed that 54a Pennington Street was just a house—not an artists' colony, or a commune, or any kind of sociological experiment. It was a fairly plainly decorated one at that. It looked like it might have been shipped straight out of an office supply catalog. Low-pile carpet. Simple furniture in flat navy blues and blacks. Nothing on the walls. Nothing, that is, until they came to a small, sunny bedroom.

"This was Peg's room," Richard said, opening the door. But Ginny didn't need to be told that. It was a miniature version of the 4th Noodle apartment. In fact, the room resembled the apartment so closely it was almost spooky. It wasn't that she had furnished it or painted it exactly the same—it was the method. The walls had been washed down in pink and then covered in an elaborate collage of . . . well, trash, really. (When Ginny's mom got annoyed with her little sister, she tended to make comments about Aunt Peg's trash-picking habit. "She's got other people's garbage all over her walls!")

But it wasn't bad, smelly trash—it was labels, bits of old magazines, candy bar wrappers. If anyone else had attempted this, the result would have been dizzying, nauseating. But Aunt Peg managed to arrange it all by color, by type style, by image, so that it all looked like it belonged together. Like it all made sense. One wall had been left collage-free, and on it hung a poster Ginny recognized. It was a French painting of a young woman standing behind a bar. It was an old picture, from the late 1800s. The woman wore an elegant blue dress, and the bar she was tending was opulent—marble, loaded down with bottles. The mirror behind her head reflected a crowd and a show. But she looked terribly, terribly bored.

"It's Manet," she said. "It's called *The Bar at the Folies-Bergère*."

"Is it?"

Richard blinked, as if he'd never noticed the poster there before. "I don't really know anything about art," he said apologetically. "It's nice, I suppose. Nice . . . colors."

Good one, Ginny thought. Now he probably thought she was some kind of art nerd who was only here because she had outgrown art-nerd camp. She only knew the name and artist of this one because Aunt Peg had had the exact same picture in her apartment, and the title and artist had been written at the bottom of the print.

Richard was still staring blankly at the poster.

"I don't really know much about it either," Ginny said. "It's okay."

"Oh. Right." He seemed a bit reassured by that. "You look exhausted. Maybe you'd like to have a rest? Again, I'm sorry, I wish I had known when . . . but you're here, so . . ."

Ginny looked at the bed, with its crazy-quilt cover. This was Aunt Peg's handiwork as well. She'd had similar items all over her apartment, all made of random, mismatched pieces of cloth. She wanted to stretch out on this bed so badly she could almost taste it.

"Well, I . . . I have to go," he said. "Maybe you'd like to come with me? I work at Harrods. The big department store. It's as good a place as any to start seeing London. Peg loved Harrods. We can sort everything out later. What do you say?"

"Sure," Ginny said, with one final, sad look at the bed. "Let's go."

Harrods

Ginny was passing in and out of thoughtful consciousness on the tube. They were stuck in the morning rush, forced to stand. The rhythm of the train lulled her. It look a lot of effort not to give in to her wobbling knees and slump into Richard.

Richard was obviously trying to make conversation, pointing out things that could be seen at each of the various stops—anything from the major (Buckingham Palace, Hyde Park) to the minor (his dentist, "a really good Thai takeaway"). His words were dribbling into the ebbing sensory mess that surrounded her. British voices swirled around her head. Her eyes flicked over the advertisements that ran along the top of the car. Though the language was the same, the meaning of many of the posters was lost on her. It seemed like every one of them was some kind of inside joke.

"You look a lot like Peg," he said, catching her attention.

This was somewhat true. They had similar hair, at least—

long and deep chocolate brown. Aunt Peg was shorter. She had a slender build and a regal bearing that made strangers assume she was a dancer. Her features were very delicate. Ginny was taller, curvier. Bigger, generally. Less delicate.

"I guess," she said.

"No. You really do. It's extraordinary. . . ." He was hanging on to an overhead strap and looking down at her with an intense stare. Something about his look managed to penetrate Ginny's exhaustion, and she found herself staring back with equal intensity. This move startled them both, and they looked away at the same time. Richard didn't speak again until they reached the next stop and informed Ginny that this was Knightsbridge. This was their stop.

They emerged onto a pulsing London street. The road was completely jammed with red buses, black cabs, tiny cars, motorcycles. . . . The sidewalks were crammed to capacity. Though her brain was still cloudy, Ginny felt a shock of energy run through her body at the sight of it all.

Richard directed her around a corner to a building that seemed to stretch on forever. It was a solid wall of golden red brick, with decorative cornices and a dome on the roof. Green awnings stretched above dozens of huge windows, each opulently displaying clothes, perfume, cosmetics, stuffed animals, even a car. Each one of these awnings was printed with the word *Harrods* in a mustard-gold script. Richard led Ginny past the windows, past the front doors and the doorman, and around to an unobtrusive nook by a large trash bin.

"This is it," Richard said, indicating the side of the building and a door marked STAFF ONLY. "We're going in through a side entrance. It gets a bit mad in here. Harrods is a big tourist destination. We get thousands and thousands of people a day."

They entered a stark white hallway with a bank of elevators. A sign on the wall next to the door listed various departments and floors. Ginny wondered if she was misreading them: Air Harrods helicopter services, Air Harrods jet aircraft, tennis racquet restringing, piano tuning, saddlery, dog coat fitting. . . .

"I just have to take care of a few things," he said. "Maybe you can walk around, have a look at the store, and meet me here in an hour or so? That door leads to the ground floor. Plenty of things to look at in Harrods."

Ginny was still stuck on "dog coat fitting."

"If you get lost," he said, "have someone call Special Services and ask for me, all right? My last name's Murphy, by the way. Ask for Mr. Murphy."

"Okay."

He punched a code into a small number pad and the door clicked open.

"It's good to have you here," he said, smiling widely. "See you in an hour."

Ginny poked her head through the doorway. A display case there featured a miniature speedboat, only big enough for a small child. It was colored olive green and had the name *Harrods* printed over the bow. The sign said: FULLY OPERATIONAL. £20,000.

And then there were people. Massive, scary throngs of people pouring in through the doors, lining up at the display cases. She stepped tentatively into the crowd and was immediately absorbed into the flow of humanity, which sucked her along. She was pushed past the cigarette lighter repair desk, through a Princess Diana memorial, into a Starbucks, and then dropped on an escalator entirely decorated in Egyptian artifacts (or really good copies, anyway).

She went up through the hieroglyphics and the statues until the river of people unloaded her into some kind of children's theater room with a Punch and Judy show. She managed to get through that room pretty much on her own, but the crowd got her again as she passed through the door into a room filled with tuxedos for babies.

Departments that made no sense were strung together in a series of large and small rooms. Every offshoot led to something weirder, and nothing appeared to be an exit. There was always just *more*. She went from a room displaying colorful kitchen appliances into a room entirely filled with pianos. From there, she was swept up by the crowd into a room of exotic pet supplies. Then a room devoted solely to women's accessories, but only ones colored light blue—purses, silk scarves, wallets, shoes. Even the walls were light blue. The crowd snagged her again— now she was in a bookstore—now back on the Egyptian escalator.

She rode all the way down and stepped off into some kind of food palace that stretched on for room after massive room devoted to every kind of food, organized as an ever–Mary Poppin-izing array of displays, great arches of peacock-patterned stained glass and sparkling brass. Decorative carts stacked with pyramids of perfect fruit. Marble counters loaded down with bricks of chocolate.

Her eyes started to water. The voices around her thrummed

in her head. The bolt of energy she'd gotten on the street had been rubbed away by all the people, burned out by all the colors. She found herself fantasizing about all the places she could rest. Under the fake wagon that held the parmesan cheese display. On the floor next to the shelves full of cocoa. Maybe here, right in the middle of everything. Maybe people would just step over her.

She managed to pull out of the crowd and get to a chocolate counter. A young woman with a short and taut blond ponytail came over to her.

"Excuse me," Ginny said, "could you call Mr. Murphy?"

"Who?" the woman asked.

"Richard Murphy?"

The woman looked highly skeptical, but she still politely took out what looked like a thousand pages of names and numbers and systematically flipped through them.

"Charles Murphy in special orders?"

"*Richard* Murphy."

Several hundred more pages. Ginny felt herself gripping the counter.

"Ah . . . here he is. Richard Murphy. And what is it I need to tell him?"

"Can you tell him it's Ginny?" she said. "Can you tell him that I need to go?"

Good Morning, England

The small alarm clock read 8:06. She was in bed, still in her clothes. It was cool, and the sky outside was a pearly gray.

She vaguely recalled Richard putting her in one of those black cabs in front of Harrods. Arriving at his house. Fumbling with keys and what seemed like six locks on the door. Getting up the stairs. Falling onto the quilt fully dressed, with her ankles hanging off the side so that her sneakers didn't get on it.

She kicked her feet. They were still hanging there off the edge of the bed.

She looked around the room. It was strange to be waking up here—not only in a different country (different country . . . everyone an entire ocean away . . . she was *not* going to panic). No, it wasn't just that. This room really felt like a moment from her past, like Aunt Peg had just walked through the room, covered in blotches of paint, humming under her breath. (Aunt Peg hummed a lot. It was kind of annoying.)

When she emerged into the hallway and peered into the kitchen, she found that Richard had changed his clothes. Now he was wearing running pants and a T-shirt.

"Morning," he said.

This made no sense.

"Morning?" she repeated.

"It's morning," he said. "You must have been exhausted. Jet lag. I shouldn't have dragged you off to Harrods yesterday, not when you were so tired."

Yesterday. Now her brain was catching up. Eight a.m. She'd lost an *entire day.*

"Sorry," she said quickly. "I'm really sorry."

"Nothing to be sorry for. Bath's all yours."

She went back to the bedroom and gathered up her things. Though the letter had told her not to bring any guidebooks, it didn't say she couldn't look at them before she left. So she had, and she'd packed exactly the way they told her to pack. Her bag was full of "neutral basics" that didn't require ironing, could be layered, and wouldn't offend anyone, anywhere. Jeans. Cargo shorts. Practical shoes. One black skirt that she didn't like. She picked out a pair of jeans and a shirt.

Once she had filled her arms with all the necessary items, Ginny suddenly felt self-conscious about being seen going into the bathroom. She poked her head out of the bedroom and, seeing that Richard had his back turned, dashed across the hall and quickly shut the door.

It was in the bathroom that Ginny fully realized that she was in a guy's house. A man's house. A kind of messy English man's house. At home, the bathrooms were crammed full of country-crafty wicker wall ornaments, and seashells, and potpourri that smelled like the Hallmark store. This room was stark blue with blue carpet and dark blue towels. No decorations. Just a little shelf full of shaving cream (unknown brand in a vaguely futuristic-looking container), a razor, a few men's Body Shop items (all tan or amber colored and serious looking—she could tell they all smelled like tree or something suitably manly).

All of her toiletries were carefully sealed up in a plastic bag, which she set on the carpet. (Wall-to-wall—plush but worn flat. Who carpeted a bathroom?) Her stuff was all pink—had she meant to buy so much pink? Pink soap, pink miniature shampoo bottle, little pink razor. Why? Why was she so pink?

She took a second to close the blind on the large bathroom window. Then she turned to the tub. She looked at the wall, then up at the ceiling.

There was no showerhead. That must be what Richard meant by "the bath" was all hers, which she had thought was just some Britishism. But it was all too real. There was a Y-shaped rubber tube. There were open suction cups on each tip of the Y part, and there was a handle on the end of the stem that looked a lot like a phone. After examining the tub and this device, Ginny determined that the Y tips were supposed to go over the two spigots, and water would come out of the phone, and some shower-like action would result.

She gave this a try.

Water shot up toward the ceiling. She quickly pointed the shower phone into the tub and jumped in. But it proved impossible to try to wash herself and juggle the shower phone, and she gave up and filled the tub. She hadn't taken a bath since she was little and felt a little stupid sitting in the water. Also, the bath was amazingly loud—every movement produced a sloshing noise that echoed embarrassingly. She tried to make her movements as conservative as possible as she washed up, but the effort was lost as soon as she had to submerge herself to wash her hair. She was pretty sure that ocean liners could be lowered into the sea and make less noise than she did.

When the drama of the bath was over, she realized that she had another, totally unexpected problem. Her hair was soaked, and she had no way of drying it. She hadn't brought a blow dryer since it wouldn't work here anyway. There was no alternative, it seemed, but to quickly bind it up in braids.

When she emerged, she found Richard all suited up in what appeared to be the same suit and tie he had on the day before.

"Hope you were all right in there," he said apologetically. "I don't have a shower."

He'd probably heard her sloshing around all the way in the kitchen.

Richard started opening cabinet doors and pointing out things that might be considered breakfast-worthy. He was clearly unprepared for her visit, as the best he could offer was a bit of leftover bread, a little jar of brown stuff called Marmite, an apple, and "whatever is in the refrigerator."

"I've got some Ribena here, if you want that," he added, taking a bottle of some kind of grape juice and setting it in front of Ginny as well. He excused himself for a moment. Ginny got a glass and poured herself some of the juice. It was warm and incredibly thick. She took a sip and gagged slightly as the intense, overly sweet syrup coated her throat.

"You're . . ." Richard was in the kitchen doorway now, watching this with an embarrassed expression. "You're supposed to mix that with water. I should have told you."

"Oh," Ginny said, swallowing hard.

"I've got to be off now," he said. "I'm sorry . . . there's been no time to talk at all. Why don't you meet me at Harrods for lunch? Let's meet at Mo's Diner at noon. If you ever get locked out, I leave a spare key wedged in the crack in the step."

He carefully walked her through the tube journey from the house to Harrods and made her repeat it back to him, then walked her through all the bus options, which was just a big jumble of numbers. Then he was gone, and Ginny was at the table alone, with her glass of syrup. She gazed at it sourly, still stung by the expression on Richard's face when he'd seen her drinking it. She picked up the bottle and examined it to see if there was any warning, any indication that it was anything but normal juice, anything that would make her behavior less freakish.

To her relief, there was nothing on the bottle that could have helped her. It said that it was something called "blackcurrant squash." It was "only 89p!" It was made in the United Kingdom. Which is where she was. She was in a kingdom far, far from home.

And who was this Richard, anyway, aside from a guy in a suit who worked in a big store? Looking around his kitchen, she decided he was definitely single. There were relatively few groceries—just things like this warm instant juice stuff. There were some clothes on the chairs nearest to the wall and a few scattered crumbs and coffee granules on the table.

Whoever he was, he'd let Aunt Peg stay long enough to decorate an entire room. It must have taken time to make the collage and sew the bedspread. She had to have been here for months.

She got up and retrieved the package. After brushing a spot clean, she laid the envelopes out on the table. She looked over each of the eleven unopened ones. Most had been decorated with some kind of picture as well as a number. The front of the next one had been painted in watercolors in the style of a Monopoly Community Chest card. Aunt Peg had created her own version of the little man in the top hat with the monocle, with a very fat and round plane going by the background. She'd even managed to sketch out letters that looked like the Monopoly typescript. They read: TO BE OPENED THE MORNING AFTER THE SUCCESSFUL COMPLETION OF ENVELOPE #2.

That required her to find out what Richard had sold the queen and getting to an ATM. She needed money anyway. All she had left was a handful of strangely shaped coins, which she hoped would be enough to get her back to Harrods.

Ginny snatched up the directions that Richard had written for her minutes before, dumped the offending juice down the sink, and headed for the door.

42

Richard and the Queen

A red bus was coming down the street in Ginny's direction. The sign on the front listed several famous-sounding destinations, including Knightsbridge, and the number matched one of the bus numbers Richard had given her. There was a small bus shelter a few feet away, and it looked like the bus planned on stopping there.

Two black poles with illuminated yellow globes on top of them marked the opening of the pedestrian crossing. Ginny ran to these, glanced to make sure the coast was clear, and started to run across the road.

Sudden honking. A big black cab whizzed past her. As Ginny jumped back, she saw something written on the road. LOOK LEFT.

"It's like they know me," she mumbled to herself.

She managed to get across the road and tried to ignore the fact that everyone on one side of the bus had just witnessed her near-death experience. She had no idea what to pay the driver. Ginny helplessly held out her little bit of remaining money and he took one of the fat coins. She went up the narrow spiral staircase in the middle of the bus. There were many seats available, and Ginny took one at the very front. The bus started to move.

It felt like she was floating. From her perspective, it looked like the bus was running over countless pedestrians and bicyclists, squashing them into oblivion. She pushed herself farther back into the seat and tried not to pay any attention to this. (Except they *had* to have just killed that guy on the cell phone. Ginny waited to feel the bump as the bus rolled over his body, but it never came.)

She looked around at the imposing facades of the stately buildings around her. The sky went from cloudy to gray in the space of a moment, and rain started hammering the wide windows in front of her. Now it looked like they were mowing down huge crowds of umbrella carriers.

She looked down at her smattering of remaining coins.

Aside from the 4th Noodle Penthouse, there was one other thing about Aunt Peg's life that had been completely consistent—she was broke. *Always.* Ginny had known this even when she was very small and wasn't supposed to know things about her relatives' finances. Her parents somehow made this fact apparent without ever coming out and saying it.

Still, it never seemed like Aunt Peg was wanting for anything. She always seemed to have enough money to take Ginny for frozen hot chocolates at Serendipity, or to buy her piles of art supplies, or to make her elaborate Halloween costumes, or to get that jar of really good caviar she bought once just because she thought Ginny should taste it. ("If you're going to do fish eggs once, do it right," she had said. It was still gross.)

Ginny wasn't sure if she believed that there was any more money waiting for her in an ATM. Maybe it would be there since it wasn't going to be *real* money—it was going to be pounds. Pounds seemed possible. Pounds sounded like they should come in the form of tiny burlap bags tied in rough string, filled with little bits of metal or shiny objects. Aunt Peg could have *that* kind of money.

It took a few tries on the escalators and a few consultations of the Harrods map to find Mo's Diner. Richard had gotten there first and was waiting in a booth. He ordered a steak, and she got the "big American-style burger!"

"I'm supposed to ask you what you sold to the queen," she said.

He smiled and dabbed some ketchup onto his steak. Ginny tried not to wince.

"My job is to take care of special orders and customers," he said, not noticing her distress over his condiment choice. "Say a star is out on a movie set and can't get their favorite chocolate, or soap, or sheets, or whatever. . . . I make arrangements to get it to them. Last year, I made sure all of Sting's Christmas hampers were properly packed. And occasionally, *occasionally*, I get to set up royal visits. We open at special times for those, and I make sure that there's someone in the necessary departments. One day, we got a call from the palace that the queen wanted to come over that evening, in just a few hours. She never does that. She's always very carefully scheduled weeks in advance. But this night she wanted to come in, and there was no one else available. So I had to take care of her."

"What did she want?" Ginny asked.

"Pants," he said, dabbing on even more ketchup. "*Underwear* pants. Big ones. Very nice ones as well, but big ones. I believe she also got some stockings, but all I could think as I wrapped them up in the tissue was, 'I'm packing up the queen's pants.' Peg always did like that story."

At Peg's name, Ginny looked up.

"It's a funny thing," he went on. "I don't know what you're meant to be doing here or how long you're supposed to stay, but you're welcome, as long as you like."

He said it very sincerely but kept his eyes trained on his steak.

"Thanks," she said. "I guess Aunt Peg asked if I could come."

"She mentioned that she wanted you to. I mailed the package. I suppose you know that?"

She didn't, but it made as much sense as anything else. Someone had to send it.

"So," Ginny said, "she was your roommate, huh?"

"Yeah. We were good mates." He pushed his steak around for a moment. "She told me a lot about you. About your family. I felt like I knew you before you ever got here."

He poured a bit more ketchup, then set the bottle down very deliberately and looked at her.

"You know, if you want to talk about it at all . . ."

"It's fine," she said. His sudden directness . . . the closeness of the topic, the *it* . . . it made her nervous.

46

"Right," he replied quickly. "Of course."

The waitress dropped a handful of forks next to their table. They both stopped to watch her pick them up.

"Is there an ATM in here anywhere?" Ginny finally asked.

"Several," he said, looking eager to take up this new topic of conversation. "I'll show you when we're done."

They were done just a few minutes later, as they both developed a sudden interest in eating very quickly. Richard showed Ginny to the ATM and returned to work, with the promise of seeing her in the evening.

To her relief, Ginny found that English ATMs looked exactly like American ones. She approached one and stuck in the card. The machine politely asked for a code.

"All right," Ginny said. "Here we go."

She entered the word *pants* into the keypad. The machine purred and showed her a few advertisements about how she could save for a home, and then it asked her what she wanted.

She had no idea what she wanted, but she had to pick something. Some number. There were lots of numbers to choose from.

Twenty pounds, please. That seemed like a good, basic kind of number.

No. She was on her own. She would need to buy things and get around, so . . .

One hundred pounds, please.

The machine asked for a moment. Ginny felt her stomach drop. Then a stack of crisp purple and blue notes (different sizes: the purple ones were large, the blue ones little) emblazoned with pictures of the queen popped out of the slot. (Now she got it. Aunt Peg's little joke also ensured that Ginny would never forget the code.) The large notes didn't fit in her wallet, so she had to crush them in.

Her balance, the machine said, was £1856. Aunt Peg had come through.

#3

Dear Ginny,

Let's get right down to business.

Today is MYSTERIOUS BENEFACTOR DAY. Why Mysterious Benefactor Day? Well, Gin, let me give you a because: because talent alone doesn't make an artist. You need a little serendipity, a little luck, a little boost. I stumbled right into someone who helped me out, and it's time to return the favor. But it's also good to be mysterious. Make someone think that wonderful things are happening to them for no reason they can see. I've always wanted to be a fairy godmother, Gin, so help me out here.

Step one: Withdraw 500 pounds from the account.

Step two: Find an artist in London whose work you like, someone you think deserves a break. This is going to require some looking around on your part. Any kind of artist--a painter, a musician, a writer, an actor.

Step three: Become A MYSTERIOUS BENEFACTOR. Buy a new invisible box for a mime, get a mile's worth of violin strings for a violinist, roll up in front of a ballet studio with a year's supply of lettuce . . . whatever you want.

Now, I think I know what you're thinking: This can't be done in a day! You are so wrong, Gin. Those are your orders. When you've successfully done this, you can open the next letter.

Love,
YOUR RUNAWAY AUNT

The Benefactor

The next morning, after reading her letter and splashing around in the tub, Ginny joined Richard at the kitchen table. He was loosely dressed—unbuttoned shirt, undone tie—and was roughly flipping through the sports section of the paper and shoving pieces of toast into his mouth.

"I have to find an artist today," she said. "Someone who needs money."

"An artist?" he said, his mouth half full. "Oh, dear. Sounds like a Peg task. I don't really know much about that stuff."

"Oh. That's okay."

"No, no," he said. "Let me think a moment. It shouldn't be hard. Giving people money can't be hard."

He munched on his toast thoughtfully for another moment.

"Hang on," he said. "We'll have a look in *Time Out*. That's what we'll do."

He reached under a pile of shirts that sat on one of the

kitchen chairs, felt around for a second, and produced a magazine. Ginny had a strange feeling that leaving laundry on the kitchen chairs was something Aunt Peg probably didn't allow when she was here. For someone who lived pretty randomly, she was a bit of a neat freak.

"They list everything in here," Richard said brightly, opening the magazine. "All kinds of movies, art events. Here's one, and right near here. Izzy's Café, Islington. Shelia Studies, paintings by Romily Mezogarden. And here's another . . . a bit strange sounding. Harry Smalls, demolition artist. That's just around the corner. If you're ready, I can walk you there."

He seemed genuinely pleased that he'd been able to come up with something.

Ginny wasn't quite ready, but she hurriedly squeezed some water from her braids and put on her sneakers. She managed to make it to the front door just a second before he did, and they walked out into the drizzly morning together.

"I have a few minutes," he said. "I'll pop in with you."

Izzy's Café was a tiny place with a juice bar. No one was there, but the girl behind the counter was making a whole pitcher of beet juice anyway. She waved a purple-stained hand at them as they came in.

A series of paintings hung in a ring around the room, and it was immediately obvious that these were the "Shelia Studies." As advertised, they were studies of some girl named Shelia. The background in Shelia's world was bright blue and everything in it was flat, including Shelia. Shelia had a large, flat head with a square chunk of yellow hair sticking up out of it. Shelia usually just stood around (*#4: Shelia Standing; #7: Shelia Standing in*

Bedroom; *#18: Shelia Standing in Road*). Sometimes, she would stand around and hold things (*#24: Shelia with Eggbeater*) or look at things (*#34: Shelia Looking at Pencil*), and then she would get tired and sit *(#9: Shelia Sitting on Box)*.

"I'm rubbish at this," Richard said, scanning the walls hopelessly. "But I'm sure you know something."

Ginny took a closer look and discovered the little cards under the pictures. She was amazed to find that Romily Mezogarden wanted £200 for each and every one of the Shelia pictures. That seemed like a lot, considering that they were really ugly and the whole thing seemed uncomfortably stalker-like.

She didn't know anything about art either. These could be the greatest pictures in the world. There were people who could tell these things. She was not one of them. Still, it seemed like she should have a slight air of competence. She was Aunt Peg's niece, after all. She got the strange feeling that somehow Richard was expecting her to know something.

"Maybe not these," she said. "I'll look at the next one."

He went with her to the next place, an installation by Harry Smalls, demolition artist, who Ginny quickly dubbed "The Half Guy." He cut things in half. All kinds of things. Half a briefcase. Half a sofa. Half a mattress. Half a tube of toothpaste. Half an old car. Ginny thought this one over, then asked herself if she really wanted to give almost a thousand dollars to a guy who had a chain saw problem.

Once they were back outside, Ginny struggled to come up with another idea.

"I'm thinking maybe one of those people who perform on the street," she said. "Where do you think I could find those?"

"Like buskers? Street musicians, people like that?"

"Right," Ginny said. "Like that."

"Try Covent Garden," he said after a moment. "Middle of London. Lots of performers. All sorts of things going on, people selling things. It has its own tube stop. You can't miss it."

"Great," she said. "I'll go there."

"It's on the way. Come on, then."

She rode with Richard in the late morning rush until he ushered her off at her stop.

There was nothing garden-like about Covent Garden. It was a large cobblestoned plaza, jammed with tourists and stalls of knickknacks. There was also no shortage of performers. She gave it her best, spending over an hour sitting on the curb, watching. Some guys juggled knives. Several guitarists of varying quality played either acoustically or through banged-up amps. A magician pulled a duck from his coat.

All she would have to do was pull the pile of bills from her pocket and drop them into any one of these hats or guitar cases and she'd be done. She could picture the scene—the astonished knife-throwers looking at the flutter of twenty-pound notes. The thought was tempting, but something told her that this wasn't right, either. She gripped the money in her pocket, balled it tight, then got up and started walking.

The sun was making more of an effort today, and the Londoners seemed to appreciate it. Ginny wandered around the stalls, wondering if she should buy Miriam a T-shirt. Then she was walking down a street full of bookstores. Then she was in a massive square (which, according to the tube stop there, was called Leicester Square) and it was five o'clock, and the streets were beginning to fill with people getting off work. Her chances of succeeding seemed to be rapidly dwindling. She was about to turn back and divvy up the money between all of the hats on Covent Garden when she noticed a large advertisement for something called Goldsmiths College, which claimed to be London's premier art college. Plus, the advertisement gave directions. It seemed worth a try.

She found herself on a city street, with a few fairly modern academic buildings scattered around. Of course, she realized, it was also summer, and evening, which meant no school and no students.

She should have thought of that before she'd come all the way down here.

She wandered around, glancing at a few flyers stuck to notice boards and walls. A few protests. Yoga classes. A few album releases. She was about to turn and give up when a flapping piece of paper caught her eye. It read: STARBUCKS: THE MUSICAL. There was a cartoon of a man diving into a coffee cup. The bottom of the flyer said that the show was written, produced, directed, and designed by someone named Keith Dobson.

Something about this just sounded promising. And it was still going on—even now, in the summer. Tickets, the flyer promised, were on sale in something called the uni. She asked a girl passing by what it was.

"The uni?" (She pronounced it *you-knee*.) "That's the student union. It's just across the road."

It took a lot of asking around to find her way through Goldsmiths' massive student union building to where they sold tickets to the show. It was like they didn't want anyone to find it: down two sets of stairs, around a corner, left at the bucket (really) to a door at the end of a hallway, where only one of two fluorescent lights worked. There was a flyer for the show stuck to the door and a pale redheaded guy visible through the nine inches of plastic window that made this a box office and not a closet. He looked up from a copy of *War and Peace*.

She figured she'd have to scream to be heard, so she just held up a finger to show that she wanted one ticket. He held up his hands and indicated eight. She dug around in her pocket and found one of the tiny five-pound notes and three of the pound coins and carefully pressed these through the slot in the plastic, and he pulled a photocopied ticket from a cigar box and passed it over to her. Then he jerked his finger, pointing her toward two red double doors at the end of the hall.

Jittery Grande

She was in a big, black basement room. It was a little damp. A few fake palm trees had been pushed off to the side. The seats were mostly empty and a few people sat on the floor or on steps in the back of the room. All in all, there were only maybe ten people in the audience. Most of them were smoking and talking to one another. She was the only person here who didn't seem to know someone else. It felt like a private party in a basement.

She was thinking about getting up and leaving just as a girl appeared in the doorway near where she had come in and flipped off the light switches. Punk music started to blast from a few scattered speakers on one side of the room. A moment later, it stopped abruptly, and a light came on in the middle of the stage.

Standing there was a guy, maybe her age or just a little older, dressed in a green kilt, a Starbucks shirt, heavy black boots, and a top hat. A fringe of light reddish hair stuck out from under the hat, brushing along the top of his shoulders. He had a wide, slightly evil grin.

"I'm Jittery Grande," he said. "I'm your host!"

He jumped closer to the audience, practically onto Ginny's feet, eliciting a short laugh from a girl sitting on the floor nearby.

"Do you like coffee?" he asked the audience.

A few assorted affirmatives and one "piss off!"

"Do you like *Starbucks* coffee?" he asked.

More insults. He seemed to like that.

"Well, then," he said, "let's get started!"

The show was about a Starbucks employee named Joe who developed a crush on a customer. There was a love song ("I Love You a Latte"), a breakup song ("Where Have You Bean?"), and a song that seemed to be some kind of a protest ("Beating the Daily Grind"). It ended tragically when she stopped drinking coffee, and he threw himself offstage into what was supposed to be the Main Bean Supply. All of this was somehow arranged by Jittery, who remained onstage the entire time, talking to the audience, telling Joe what to do, and holding up signs that gave statistics on how the global economy was wrecking the environment.

Ginny had seen enough shows in her lifetime to know that this wasn't a very *good* show. It didn't actually make any sense. There were a lot of random things going on, like a guy who sometimes rode through the scene on a bike for no reason that Ginny could figure. And at one point, there was a shooting in the background, but the guy who got shot just kept on singing, so his injuries obviously weren't that bad.

Despite all of that, Ginny found herself quickly and totally engrossed—and she knew why. She had a thing for performers.

She always had. It probably had something to do with all of the performances Aunt Peg had taken her to as a kid. She had always been amazed that there were people who weren't afraid of getting up in front of crowds and just . . . talking. Or singing, dancing, telling jokes. Flaunting themselves with no embarrassment.

Jittery wasn't a particularly good singer, but this didn't stop him from belting away. He jumped around the stage. He prowled through the audience. He *owned* the place.

When it was all over, she picked up a program someone had left on the seat next to her and read it. Keith Dobson—director, writer, producer—also happened to play Jittery Grande.

Keith Dobson was her artist. And she had 492 little burlap sacks to give to him.

The next morning, as she made her way down the long linoleum hallway to the little ticket closet, Ginny realized that her shoes were squeaky. *Really* squeaky.

She stopped and looked down at her sneakers. There they were, white with pink stripes, poking out below the heavy olive drab of her cargo shorts. She remembered the exact sentence from the travel guide that had caused her to choose these shoes out of all possible shoes: "You'll be doing a lot of walking in Europe, so make sure to bring comfortable walking shoes! Sneakers are universally acceptable, and white ones will keep you cool in the summer."

She hated that sentence now. Hated it, and the person who wrote it. These shoes made her stand out—and not just because of the noise. White sneakers were the Official Shoe of Tourists. This was London, and the real Londoners wore skinny heels or Euroshoes in weird colors or coffee-colored leather boots. . . .

And shorts. No one wore shorts either.

This had to be why Aunt Peg said that she couldn't have any guidebooks. She'd looked in one, and it had made her a squeaky, white-shoed freak.

Anyway (*squeak, squeak*), what was she supposed to do? She couldn't just shove (*squeak*) the money at the ticket guy and run off. Well, she could, but then there was no way of making sure it would get to him. She could put it in an envelope and address it to Jittery (or Keith), but that didn't seem right either.

She would just buy the tickets quickly and anonymously. It was the best way. Tickets were eight pounds. Ginny quickly did the math in her head, then strode up to the window.

"I'll take sixty-two tickets, please," she said.

The guy looked up from his copy of *War and Peace*. He had come pretty far in one day, Ginny noticed. The Simpsons shirt was the same, though.

"You what?"

He had one of those stuffed-up-nose voices, which made the question extra questioning.

"Can I have sixty-two?" she asked, her own voice inadvertently dropping.

"We only have twenty-five seats," he said. "And that's with people sitting on the floor."

"Oh. Sorry. I'll just take . . . what can I have?"

He lifted the lid of a cigar box on the counter and thumbed through the two stubs inside. Then he shut it decisively.

"You can have twenty-three."

"Okay," Ginny said, fumbling through the wad of pound notes. "I'll take them."

"What do you want twenty-three tickets for?" he asked as he snapped a rubber band from a pile and counted them out.

"Just, people."

There was a dripping noise somewhere in the hall. It seemed to suddenly get very loud.

"Well, I'm not arguing," he said after a moment. "You a student?"

"Not here."

"Anywhere."

"High school? In New Jersey?"

"Student discount, then. Five pounds each." He pulled out a calculator and punched in the numbers. "That'll be one hundred and fifteen pounds."

This discount left Ginny with a problem. She'd need more tickets. Lots more.

"How many can I have for tomorrow?" she asked.

"What?"

"How many for tomorrow?"

"We haven't sold any."

"I'll take them all."

He eyed her as she slipped £125 through the slice in the plastic, and he slid over twenty-five tickets.

"What about the next night?"

He got up and pressed his face against the window to look at her. He was really pale. She guessed that was what happened if you spent the summer in a basement, sitting in a closet next to a bucket.

"Who are you *with*?" he asked.

"Just . . . me."

"Is this some kind of joke, then?"

"No."

He retracted and sat back on his stool.

"No shows Thursday," he said, his snufflyness increasing. "The martial arts club is giving a belt test in the space."

"Friday?"

"That's the last show," he said. "We've sold three of those. You can have the other twenty-two."

One hundred ten pounds more passed through the cut in the plastic.

Ginny thanked him and stepped over the bucket and counted out her tickets and remaining money. Seventy tickets. One hundred forty-two more pounds to *benefact*.

Behind her, she heard a noise. The liberated ticket seller stepped out of his closet, nodded to her, and carried the cigar box of money down the hall, upstairs, and into the light of day. She noticed that a hastily scrawled sign had appeared in the window. It read: SOLD OUT, FOREVER.

Bright Ideas

It was only when she was back up on the street with all of the tickets to Keith's show in her grasp that Ginny realized that there was a flaw in her plan. Yes, she'd given him money—sort of. But now no one would see him perform, starting immediately. She'd purchased him, lock, stock, and barrel.

She went into such a panic that she forgot where the tube stop was and circled the same block three times, and when she finally did find it, there was only one place she could think to go.

Back to Harrods. Back to Richard. Back to the same chocolate counter in the food hall because at least she knew they had a phone and the guide there. Richard dutifully came down and escorted her to the Krispy Kreme. (Yes, Harrods had a Krispy Kreme. This store really did have it all.)

"If you had to give out seventy tickets to a show called *Starbucks: The Musical*," Ginny began, breaking her cruller in two, "where would you go?"

Richard stopped stirring his coffee and looked up.

"I can't say it's ever come up," he said.

"But if it did," she said.

"I suppose I'd go to the place where people were waiting around trying to get into shows," he said. "Have you actually purchased seventy tickets to something called *Starbucks: The Musical*?"

Ginny decided it was probably better not to answer that question.

"Where would people be looking for tickets?" she asked.

"The West End. You weren't far from there yesterday. Covent Garden, Leister Square—that's the area. It's where all the theaters are, like Broadway. But I'm not sure how successful you'll be. Still, if they're free . . ."

The West End was not as bright and in-your-face as Broadway. It lacked the three-story-high billboards that sparkled and revolved and had gold fringe. There were no massive, illuminated cups of ramen noodles, no skyscrapers. It was much more subdued, with only a few posters and signs marking out the territory. The theaters were stark, serious-looking places.

She immediately knew this was not going to work.

For a start, she was American, and she looked like a tourist, and it kept starting to rain and then stopping. Plus, the tickets weren't the official computerized kind—they were just unevenly cut photocopies. How was she supposed to show people what the show was, where it was, what it was about? And who was going to want to know about *Starbucks: The Musical* when they were waiting in line to get tickets for *Les Misérables* or *Phantom of the Opera* or *Chitty Chitty Bang Bang* or some other normal

66

show at a normal theater that sold commemorative sweatshirts and mugs?

She stationed herself near a massive brick theater off Leister Square, right by a kiosk filled with theater information. For the next hour or so, she just stood there, biting at her lower lip, clutching the tickets. She occasionally stepped forward when someone lingered by the posters, but she couldn't manage to coax herself forward to try to convince them to go and see the show.

By three o'clock, she had only managed to give away six tickets, all of them to a group of Japanese girls who accepted them politely and appeared to have no idea what they had just taken. And she'd only spoken to them because she had a pretty good idea that they had no idea what she was saying.

She dragged herself back across town to Goldsmiths. At least there she could point to the building and say, "The show's in there." An hour in front of the uni produced no results at all, until she turned to find herself face-to-face with a guy who had to be about her age. He was black, with short dreadlocks and sleek rimless glasses.

"Want to go see this show tonight?" she asked, pointing at the flyer with the dive-bombing coffee cup. "It's really good. I have free tickets."

He looked at the flyer, then at her.

"Free tickets?"

"It's a special promotion," she said.

"Is it?"

"Yes."

"What kind of a promotion?"

"A . . . special one. A free one."

"For what?"

"Just to get people to go."

"Right," he said slowly. "Can't. Busy tonight. But I'll keep it in mind, yeah?"

He gave her a lingering glance before going inside. That was as close as she got to success.

She sank down onto the bench at the bus stop and pulled out her notebook.

June 25
7:15 p.m.

Dear Miriam,

I have always been kind of proud that I have never lost it over a guy. I have never been one of those people who freaked out in the bathroom or did something lame like

1. *making a mock-suicide attempt by taking an entire bottle of vitamin C (Grace Partey, tenth grade)*
2. *failing chem by repeatedly skipping class to make out behind the cafeteria Dumpster (Joan Fassel, eleventh grade)*
3. *claiming sudden interest in Latin culture and switching from French II to Spanish I to be in same class as a hot freshman, only to get put in a different period (Allison Smart, tenth grade)*
4. *refusing to break up with a boyfriend (Alex Webber) even when he was arrested for setting fire to three sheds in his development and had to be put under observation in a mental hospital (Catie Bender, student council VP, valedictorian, twelfth grade)*

Clearly, hormones do not help our IQ.

I have always been very whatever about the whole thing. The guys I would have liked were just totally unattainable, so, given the choice between making a huge effort for guys I wasn't really interested in or being an independent human being (hanging out with my friends, making plans to escape New Jersey, injuring myself on household appliances), I decided to be an independent creature.

I know you think that I'm due for a "major romantic breakthrough" anytime now, preferably before I leave high school. And you know I think you need "major hormone therapy" because you excel at obsessing. You were obsessed with Paul all last summer. I mean, I love you dearly, but you do.

But just to make you feel better, I'll tell you something:

I am kind of sort of interested in someone who could never, ever like me. His name is Keith. He does not know me.

And before you even start with the "Of course he'll like you! You're so great!" just put it in park for a second. I know that he can't. Why? Because he is

1. a good-looking British guy
2. who is an actor
3. and who is also in college
4. in London, where he wrote a play
5. which I have just purchased ALL OF THE TICKETS FOR because of this letter thing and have only managed to give away SIX of them.

But just for fun, let's review my romantic history, shall we?

1. Den Waters. Made out with him exactly three times, all three of which he did the scary lizard-tongue thing and thanked me afterward.

2. Mike Riskus, who I obsessed over for two years and never even spoke to until right before Christmas last year. He was behind me in trig, and he asked, "Which problem set do we have to do?" And I said, "The one on page 85." And he said, "Thanks." I lived on that for MONTHS.

So, as you can see, my chances are incredibly good, given my wide appeal and experience.

Enclosed you will find a copy of the program from Keith's show.

I miss you so much it's giving me a pain in my pancreas. But you know that.

Love,
Ginny

The Hooligan and the Pineapple

Only three people showed. Since two people had already purchased tickets before Ginny got there and she had used one herself, this meant that absolutely *no one* she had given tickets to had come. Her Japanese girls had let her down.

The result of this was that the cast of *Starbucks: The Musical* outnumbered the audience, and Jittery seemed very aware of the fact. That might have been the reason he decided to skip intermission and keep right on going, eliminating any chance of letting his audience escape. For his part, Keith didn't seem to mind at all that hardly anyone was there. He took the opportunity to dive into the seats and even to climb one of the fake palm trees that sat on the side of the room.

At the end, as Ginny leapt up to make her escape, Jittery suddenly jumped down off the stage as she was reaching down to get her bag. He dropped into the empty seat next to her.

"Special promotion, eh?" he said. "What was that about?"

Ginny had heard tales of people being tongue-tied, of opening their mouths to find themselves incapable of any speech. She never thought that was literal. She always thought that was just another way of saying they couldn't think of anything good to say.

Well, she was wrong. You could lose the ability to speak. She felt it right at the top of her throat—a little tug, like the closing of a drawstring bag.

"So tell me," he said, "why did you buy three hundred quid worth of tickets and then try to give them away on the street?"

She opened her mouth. Again, nothing. He folded his arms over his chest, looking like he was prepared to wait forever for an explanation.

Speak! she screamed to herself. *Speak, dammit!*

He shook his head and ran his hand over his hair until it stuck up in high, staticky strands.

"I'm Keith," he said, "and you're . . . clearly mad, but what's your name?"

Okay. Her name. She could handle that.

"Ginny," she said. "Virginia."

Only one name was really necessary. Why had she given two?

"American, yeah?" he asked.

A nod.

"Named after a state?"

Another nod, even though it wasn't true. She was named after her grandmother. But now that she thought of it, it was technically true. She was named after a state. She had the most ridiculously American name ever.

"Well, Mad Ginny Virginia from America, I guess I owe you

a drink since you've made me the first person in all of recorded history to sell this place out."

"I am?"

Keith got up and went over to one of the fake palm trees. He pulled a tattered canvas bag from behind it.

"So you want to go, then?" he asked, tearing off the Starbucks shirt and replacing it with a graying white T-shirt.

"Where?"

"To the pub."

"I've never been to a pub."

"Never been to a pub? Well, then. You'd better come along. This is England. That's what we do here. We go to pubs."

He reached behind once again and retrieved an old denim jacket. The kilt he left on.

"Come on," he said, gesturing to her as if he was trying to coax a shy animal out from under a sofa. "Let's go. You want to go, yes?"

Ginny felt herself getting up and numbly following Keith out of the room.

The night had become misty. The glowing yellow orbs of the crossing lights and the car headlights cut strange patterns through the fog. Keith walked briskly, his hands buried in his pockets. He occasionally glanced over his shoulder to make sure Ginny was still with him. She was just a pace or two behind.

"You don't have to follow me," he said. "We're a very advanced country. Girls can walk beside men, go to school, everything."

Ginny tentatively stepped beside him and hurried to keep up with his long stride. There were so many pubs. They were everywhere. Pubs with nice English names like The Court in

Session and The Old Ship. Pretty pubs painted in bright colors with carefully made wooden signs. Keith walked past all these to a shabbier-looking place where people stood out on the sidewalk with big pints of beer.

"Here we are," he said. "The Friend in Need. Discounts for students."

"Wait," she said, grabbing his arm. "I'm . . . in high school."

"What does that mean?"

"I'm only seventeen," she whispered. "I don't think I'm legal."

"You're American. You'll be fine. Just act like you belong and no one will say a word."

"Are you sure?"

"I started getting into pubs when I was thirteen," he said. "I'm sure."

"But you're legal now?"

"I'm nineteen."

"And that's legal here, right?"

"It's not just legal," he said. "It's mandatory. Come on."

Ginny couldn't even see the bar from where they were. There was a solid wall of people guarding it and a haze of smoke hanging over it, as if it had its very own weather.

"What are you having?" Keith asked. "I'll go and get it. You try to find somewhere to stand."

She ordered the only thing she knew—something that was conveniently written on a huge mirror on the wall.

"Guinness?"

"Right."

Keith threw himself into the crowd and was absorbed. Ginny squeezed in between a clump of guys in brightly colored soccer shirts who were standing along a little ledge. They kept punching one another. Ginny backed as far into the wall as she could go, but she was sure they would still manage to hit her. There was nowhere else to stand, though. She pressed herself in close and examined the sticky rings on the wood shelf and the ashy remnants in the ashtrays. An old Spice Girls song started playing, and the hitting guys began to do a hit dance that brought them even closer to Ginny.

Keith found her there a few minutes later. He carried a pint glass full of a very dark liquid that was coughing up tiny brass-colored bubbles. There was a thin layer of cloudy foam on top. He passed her the glass. It was heavy. She had a brief flash of the thick, warm Ribena and shuddered. For himself, Keith had gotten a Coke. He glanced behind him and placed himself between the dancing guys and Ginny.

"Don't drink," he explained, seeing her staring at the soda. "I fulfilled my quota when I was sixteen. The government issued me a special card." He fixed her again with his unwavering stare. His eyes were very green, with a kind of gold starburst at the center that was just a little off-putting and intense.

"So, are you going to tell me why you did this strange thing or not?" he asked.

"I . . . just wanted to."

"You just *wanted* to buy out the show for the week? Because you couldn't get tickets for the London Eye or something?"

"What's the London Eye?"

"The bloody great Ferris wheel across from Parliament that all the normal tourists go to," he said, leaning back and eyeing her curiously. "How long have you been here?"

"Three days."

"Have you seen Parliament? The Tower?"

"No . . ."

"But you managed to find my show in the basement of Goldsmiths."

She sipped her Guinness to buy herself a second before answering, then tried not to wince or spit. Ginny had never tasted tree bark, but this was what she imagined it would be like if you ran it through a juicer.

"I got a little inheritance," she finally said. "And I wanted to spend some of it on something I thought was really worth it."

Not totally a lie.

"So, you're rich?" he said. "Good to know. Me, well, I'm not rich. I'm a hooligan."

Before he began setting the names of coffee drinks to music, Keith had led a very interesting life. In fact, Ginny soon found out, he spent the ages of thirteen to seventeen being a parent's worst nightmare. His career began with crawling over the fence to the garden of the local pub and begging for drinks or telling jokes for them. Then he figured out how to lock himself into his local at night (by hiding in an under-used cupboard) and get enough alcohol for himself and his friends. The owners got so sick of being robbed that they gave up and hired him under the table.

There followed a few years of breaking things for no reason and setting the occasional small fire. He fondly recalled razor blading the word *wanker* into the side of his schoolmaster's car so that the message would show up in a few weeks, after it rained and rusted. He decided to try stealing. At first, he stole little things—candy bars, newspapers. He moved up to small appliances and electronics. It finally ended for him after he broke into a takeout shop and was arrested for grand theft chicken kebab.

After that, he decided to turn his life around. He created a short documentary film called *How I Used to Steal and Do Other Bad Things*. He sent this away to Goldsmiths, and they thought enough of it to accept him and even give him a grant for "special artistic merit." And now he was here, creating plays about coffee.

He stopped talking long enough to notice that she wasn't drinking her Guinness at all.

"Here," he said, grabbing the glass and finishing off the remainder in one long gulp.

"I thought you said you don't drink."

"That's not drinking," he said dismissively. "I meant *drink*."

"Oh."

"Listen," he said, moving closer, "as you've effectively paid for the entire show—and cheers for that—I might as well tell you this. I'm taking it to the Fringe Festival, in Edinburgh. You know the Fringe?"

"Not really," Ginny said.

"It's pretty much *the* biggest alternative theater festival in the world," he said. "Lots of celebrities and famous shows have come out of it. Took me forever to get the school to pay to send us up there, but I did it."

She nodded.

"So," he said, "I take it you'll be coming to the show again?"

She nodded again.

"I've got to pack everything up after the show tomorrow and move it out for the night," he said. "Maybe you'd like to join in."

"I'm not sure what to do with the rest of the tickets. . . ."

Keith smiled confidently.

"Now that you've paid for them, they'll be easy to unload. There aren't a lot of people around since it's June, but the international office will take anything free. And the foreign students are usually still here, wandering around."

He looked down at her hands. She was clutching at her empty glass.

"Come on," he said. "I'll walk you to the tube."

They left the smoke of the bar and stepped back into the fog. Keith walked her along a different route, one that she would never have been able to find on her own, to the glowing red circle with the bar cutting through it that read underground.

"So, you'll be back tomorrow?" he asked.

"Yeah," she said. "Tomorrow."

She fed the ticket eater and passed through the clacking gate, descending down into the white-tiled tube station. When she got to the platform, she saw that there was a pineapple sitting on the rails of the tracks. A whole pineapple in perfect condition. Ginny stood on the very edge of the platform and looked down at it.

It was hard to figure out how a pineapple could end up in a situation like that.

She felt the whoosh of wind that she now knew accompanied the approach of the train. Any second now it would come blasting through the tunnel and cross right over this spot.

"If the pineapple makes it," she said to herself, "he likes me."

The white nose of the train appeared. She stepped away from the edge, let the train go, and waited for it to pass away.

She looked down. The pineapple wasn't broken or whole. It was simply gone.

The Not-so-Mysterious Benefactor

Discovery: It was possible to take apart a fake palm tree and fit it in a car. In fact, it was possible to take apart a whole set and get it in a car. A *little* car. A little, white, very dirty Volkswagen. This is how they were "unloading" *Starbucks: The Musical*.

"You may be asking yourself, 'Why is Keith taking these?'" Keith said as he shoved the fronds down into the trunk. "'Why, he doesn't even use these in the show.'"

"I kind of wondered," Ginny said. (She'd wondered a lot as she'd been dragging one of them down the basement hallway, actually. They were heavy.)

"Well, I did for a while," Keith said, looking at the underside of the car and how it was sinking low to the ground under the weight. "I wrote them out. But I have to make sure no one nicks them since the school paid for them. I mean, fake palm trees. Come on. These beat orange traffic cones any day of the week. These things are a prize."

He looked down at the pile of costumes that was still on the sidewalk.

"You get in and I'll pack this stuff around you," he said.

Ginny was duly stuffed in (on the wrong side), and Keith got in on her right. The car didn't look so good from the outside, but apparently its insides were in perfect working order. As soon as Keith hit the gas, it sprang to life and rocketed to the corner of the street. It squealed slightly as he took the corner and plunged into the traffic on the main road, barely missing being knocked out of the way by a double-decker bus.

She could tell Keith was one of those guys who loved to drive—he switched through the gears with great intensity and as often as humanly possible and zigzagged his way through the congestion. A black cab was suddenly within inches of them. Ginny was face-to-face with a rather surprised-looking couple, who pointed at her fearfully.

"Aren't we a little close?" she said as Keith angled the car even closer to the cab in an attempt to change lanes.

"He'll move over," Keith said lightly.

They drove through part of Essex Road that Ginny knew.

"I'm staying around here," she said.

"In Islington? Who with?"

"A friend of my aunt's."

"I'm surprised," he said. "Thought you were in a big hotel somewhere since you're an heiress or something."

Keith turned down an endless sequence of tiny, dark roads full of houses and anonymous apartment blocks, past brightly fluorescent fish-and-chip shops. Posters and ads were glued to every surface, advertising reggae albums and Indian music. Ginny found herself automatically marking the route in her mind, tracing a pattern of signs, posters, pubs, houses. Not that she would ever come here again, of course. It was just habit.

They finally stopped on an unlit street with a long row of gray stone houses. He swerved the car and parked at an angle to the curb. There were a lot of wrappers along the sidewalks and bottles in the little yards. A few of the houses were clearly unoccupied, with boards over the windows and signs pasted on the doors.

Keith came around and opened her door, then pulled out all of the things that wedged her in. He opened the front gate of one of the houses and walked up to a bright red door with a yellow plastic window panel. They unloaded the sloppily packed boxes and bags bit by bit. Once inside, they passed a kitchen and went right to a dark set of stairs, which Keith went up without switching on the light.

At the top of the stairs, there was a strong smell of old cigarette smoke. Many objects were stuffed onto the landing—a crammed bookcase with a skull on top, a hat stand draped with shoes, a pile of clothes. He kicked these aside and opened the door they sat in front of.

"My room," Keith said with a grin.

Most of the room was red. The carpet was brick red. The saggy sofa was red. The multiple bean bags on the floor were red and black. Flyers for who knew how many student plays covered the walls, along with posters for Japanese animation and comic books. The furniture consisted of plastic packing crates, with the occasional board laid across to make a shelf or table. Books and DVDs were piled everywhere.

"It *is* her," a voice said.

She turned to face the guy she had attempted to give a ticket to outside the uni—the one with the dreadlocks and the rimless glasses. He was smiling knowingly. Behind him was a blond girl, rail thin, who didn't look very happy. Her arms poked out of the stylishly shredded shoulders of her black T-shirt like two white pencils. Her eyes were round and deeply colored, and she had a pout. Her white-blond hair looked over-processed to the point of being straw-like and visibly fragile. Yet somehow this damage complemented the wild, sophisticated way she piled it on top of her head.

Automatically, Ginny looked down at herself—at her long green khaki cargo shorts, the same sneakers, her T-shirt and tiny hoodie. The tourist clothes were even more painful than usual.

"This is Ginny," Keith said. "I think you met David. David is my flatmate. And that's Fiona."

"Oh," Fiona said. "Are you *working* on the show?"

It was a reasonable enough question, but Ginny detected an insult buried in it somewhere. She was strangely sure that whatever she said was going to cause Fiona to burst out laughing. Her stomach instantly knotted, and she tried to think of a snappy comeback. After about twenty seconds of thinking about the answer, she finally came up with the knife-sharp, "I don't know."

Fiona twisted her lips into a wan smile. She looked Ginny up and down, her eyes settling on the cargo shorts and then on a long, thin cut that ran across Ginny's knee. (Packing accident. Late night. Stepladder miscalculation while getting some things out of the top of the closet.)

"We're going out," David said. "See you later."

"They've been fighting," Keith said when they were gone. "There's a shock."

"How do you know?"

"Because," he said, dumping out a box of Starbucks cups onto the floor. "That's what they do. They fight. And fight. And fight and fight and fight."

"Why?"

"Well, the short version would involve me using a word for her that Americans tend to find very offensive. The long version is that David wants to leave university and go to cooking school. He's gotten in, has a grant and everything. That's his dream. But Fiona wants him to go to Spain with her."

"Spain?"

"She's going to work as a rep," he said. "A tour guide, basically. She wants him to go, even though he needs to be here. But he'll go because he does everything she tells him to. We used to be good mates, but not anymore. It's all about Fiona now."

He shook his head, and Ginny got the feeling that this wasn't just talk—he seemed really bothered by it. But she was still caught up on the fact that Fiona was going to work in Spain. Who just decided they were going to work in Spain? Ginny hadn't even been allowed to get a job until last summer, and that was only at the SnappyDrug down the street. One entire painful summer of stocking razor refills and asking people if they wanted to sign up for the SnappyCard. And here was Fiona, who couldn't be much older than she was, running off to sunny Spain. Ginny tried to imagine that conversation. *I'm so sick of the mall. . . . Think I'll go get a job at that Gap in Madrid.*

Everyone else's life was more interesting than hers.

"She's pretty," Ginny said.

She had no idea why she said this. It was true, more or less. Fiona was elegant and striking. (Okay, she looked a little like she had recently been raised from the dead—bony, shock-white hair, shredded clothes—but in a *good way,* of course.)

"She looks like a cotton swab," Keith said dismissively. "She has no known personality and horrible taste in music. You should hear the utter crap she plays when she's here. You, however, have taste."

The switch in topic caught Ginny off guard.

"So," he said, "what was it about my show that made you want to buy up all the tickets? Was it that you wanted me all to yourself?"

Not surprisingly, she couldn't speak. This wasn't just her normal nervous reaction—it was because Keith had slid over on his knees and was now leaning over his coffee table box, his face only a foot or so from hers.

"That's it," he said. "Isn't it? Command performance?"

He was smiling now. There was some kind of dare in his eyes. And for some reason, the only impulse Ginny had was to reach into her pocket, clutch the money in a tight grip, and drop it on the table. It slowly unballed itself, like a small purple monster that had just hatched. Little tiny pictures of the queen sprouted everywhere.

"What's this?" he asked.

"It's for your show," she said. "Or whatever. Another show. It's just for you."

He sat back on his heels and looked at her.

"You're just giving me . . ." He picked up the money, flattened it out, and counted it. "One hundred and forty pounds?"

"Oh . . ." She reached into her pocket and fished out two pound coins. It had to be one hundred forty-two. As she reached for the table to add these to the pile, she realized that the entire atmosphere in the room had just changed. Whatever conversation they might have been going to have was now canceled. Her strange, sudden gesture had shorted it out.

Clunk. Clunk. She added the two pounds.

Silence followed.

"I should probably get back," she said quietly. "I know the way."

Keith opened his mouth to speak, then rubbed at his lips with the back of his hand, as if wiping a comment away.

"Let me drive you," he said. "I don't think you should go back by yourself."

They didn't speak on the ride. Keith turned the radio up loud. As soon as she was on the sidewalk in front of Richard's house, she said her goodbyes and got out as quickly as she could.

Her heart was going to explode. It was going to blast itself out of her chest and land on the sidewalk like a heaving, desperate fish. It would keep beating as long as it could, bouncing along the discarded wrappers and cigarette butts until it had calmed itself down. Then she'd go and get it and reinstall it. She saw the whole thing very clearly. Much more clearly than she could picture what had just happened to her.

Why . . . why in the middle of what was possibly her first real romantic moment . . . had she decided that the correct response was to throw a handful of money on the table? Sweaty, balled-up money and coins? And then ask to leave?

Miriam was going to kill her. Either that or she was going to haul her off to the home for the incurably stupid and romantically hopeless and leave her there forever. And that was fine. That was where she belonged. She could live with her own kind there.

She looked up at Richard's windows. The lights were off. He had gone to bed early. If he had been awake, she might have even talked this over with him. Maybe he could reassure her, explain a way to undo what she had just done. But he was asleep.

She dug the keys out of the crack in the step, wrestled with the locks, and let herself inside. She went to her room and, without switching on any lights, dug the packet of envelopes out of the front of her bag and pulled out the top one. She held it up to the streetlight's glow coming in through the window. This next letter was covered in a pen-and-ink drawing of a castle high on a hill and the small figure of a girl on a path at its base.

"Okay," Ginny said softly. "Forget it. Moving on. What's next?"

#4

Dear Gin,

Ever see one of those kung fu movies where the student travels to the remote outpost where the Master lives?

Maybe not. I only have because my sophomore-year roommate was kung fu obsessed. But you get the idea--Harry Potter goes to Hogwarts, Luke Skywalker goes to Yoda. That's what I'm talking about. The student goes off to get <u>schooled</u>.

I did it myself. After a few months in London, I decided to go and meet my idol, the painter Mari Adams. I'd wanted to meet her my entire life. My dorm room in college was covered in pictures of her work. (And pictures of her. She's very . . . distinctive.)

I don't know exactly what made me do it. I knew I needed help with my art, and I suddenly realized that she wasn't that far away. Mari lives in Edinburgh, which is grand and spooky. Edinburgh Castle is a thousand years old or so and sits high up smack in the middle of the city on a big rock called The Mound. The entire city is ancient and strange, full of twisted little alleys called wynds. Murders, ghosts, political intrigue . . . these things permeate Edinburgh.

So I got on a train and went there. And she let me in. She even let me stay for a few days.

I want you to meet her too.

That's the entire task. I don't need to be more specific. You don't need to ask her anything. Mari is the Master, Gin, and she'll know what you need even if you don't. Her kung fu is that powerful. Trust me on this one. School is in session!

Love,
YOUR RUNAWAY AUNT

The Runner

Some people believe that they are guided by forces, that the universe cuts paths for them through the dense forest of life, showing them where to go. Ginny did not believe for a second that the whole universe was bending itself to her will. She did, however, entertain a slightly more specific and far-fetched idea—Aunt Peg had done this. She had known the unknowable. She was sending Ginny to the very place that Keith had to go to anyway to work out some details for his show.

This sometimes happened with Aunt Peg. She had a weird way of knowing things, an uncanny sense of timing. When Ginny was a kid, Aunt Peg had always managed to call whenever Ginny needed her: when she had a fight with her parents, whenever she was sick, when she needed advice. So, it wasn't a complete shock that she would have somehow plotted for Ginny to go to Edinburgh, that she would have known that

Ginny would somehow blow the whole thing with the money and give her a second chance.

But did this really *mean* anything? Sure, in a purely hypothetical sense, she could even ask him if he wanted to go with her. If she were someone other than herself, that was. Miriam would do it. Lots of people would do it. She wouldn't. She wanted to, more than anything, but she wouldn't.

For a start, the mysterious benefactor task was done. She had no possible excuse for seeing Keith. Plus, she'd already made things weird with the money. And besides . . . how did you just invite someone to *go to another country with you*? (Even if it wasn't really that much of another country. It sounded like going to Canada. Not that big of a deal. Not like David and Fiona and the whole Spain thing.)

She spent the entire day at the house, debating the issue with herself. First, she watched TV. British television seemed to consist mostly of makeover shows. Garden makeovers. Fashion makeovers. House makeovers. Everything relating to change. It seemed like a hint. Change something. Make a move.

She turned off the television and looked around the living room.

She would clean, that's what she would do. Cleaning often relaxed her. She did the dishes, brushed the crumbs off the table and chairs, folded the clothes . . . anything she could think of. She spent a good half hour examining the strange machine with the small glass window and the alphabetical dial that was under the counter in the kitchen. At first, it looked like a very odd oven. It took her a while to realize it was a washing machine.

By five o'clock, the feeling wouldn't leave her. That was when

Richard called to say he would be home late. She couldn't sit anymore.

She would just walk. She would walk just to prove to herself that she had learned the way there. It wasn't far. She would walk there, look at the house, and then walk back. Then at least she could tell herself she had gone. It was pathetic, but it was better than nothing.

She wrote a quick note to Richard and headed out. She carefully retraced the route as best she could. Newsagents . . . yellow cones in the middle of the road . . . the zigzagging lines in the street . . . it was all there, somewhere in her head. But soon, the houses all looked the same. They all looked like Keith's house.

She turned a corner and got the sign she needed—namely, David. He was on the sidewalk, clutching his cell phone against his head. He was pacing back and forth in front of the gate and he didn't sound very happy. He just kept saying "no" and "fine" over and over in a way that seemed very ominous.

Ginny was close to the house by the time she realized it was him. She thought about backing away and waiting until he'd gone back inside, but he'd seen her approach. She couldn't just run. That would be weird. She could only keep walking, slowly, cautiously, toward him. As Ginny reached the gate, he went silent. Then he hung up with an angry, snapping gesture and sat down on the low front garden wall and put his head in his hands.

"Hi?" she said.

"That's it." He shook his head. "I'm not going. I told her. I told her I don't want to go to Spain."

"Oh," Ginny said. "Well. Good. For you."

"Yeah," he said, nodding heavily. "It is good. I mean, I've got to start my life here, don't I?"

"Right."

David nodded once more, then broke down into heaving sobs. There was a rustling noise above, and Ginny saw the crooked black blinds on Keith's window rocking back and forth. A moment later, he was down on the sidewalk with them. Keith glanced over at Ginny. She could see his confusion at the two things in front of him—the fact that she was there and that his roommate was dissolving in tears in front of his own house. For a second, she actually felt guilty, until she remembered that this wasn't her fault.

"Right," Keith said, striding over to his car and opening the passenger door. "Get in. Come on."

Ginny wasn't sure who he was talking to. Neither was David. They looked at each other.

"Both of you," Keith said. "Brick Lane time."

A few minutes later, she was part of this little group, speeding deeper into East London, where the houses got a little grayer and the signs were written in curvy, totally unknown languages. Indian restaurants lined both sides of the street, and even the air was permeated with the odors of heavy spices, and they all seemed to be open, even at midnight. Colorful lights were strung from building to building, and hawkers stood in doorways, offering free beer or snacks to whoever would come inside. Keith, however, knew exactly where he was going and guided them to a small, very neat little restaurant where there seemed to be four waiters for every customer.

Ginny wasn't hungry, but she felt the need to participate. She had no idea what to order, though.

"I guess I'll have what you're having," she said to Keith.

"If you had what we're having, you'd die," Keith said. "Try the mild curry."

She decided not to challenge him on that one.

Keith ordered a whole list of foods, and soon their table was covered in bread baskets full of big flat things that they called papadams. There was a selection of vividly colored chutneys with large pieces of hot pepper floating in them, and beers. As soon as she saw the spread, Ginny understood. Keith was giving David a tragedy meal. She did the same thing with Miriam when she broke up with Paul last summer, except that her version involved a half gallon of Breyers, a box of Little Debbie snack cakes, and a six-pack of blue raspberry soda. Guys would never be satisfied with that kind of comfort. If they were going to have a tragedy meal, they had to make sure there was a painful, masculine component to it.

Keith was talking a mile a minute. He started by telling a story about how he and his "mate Iggy" liked to show up at girls' houses with their trousers on fire. (A trick, he explained in detail, that involved spraying the pants with an aerosol, like Lysol, then lighting the fumes, which then created fiery clouds just on the surface of the pants, which could be put out, provided you dropped to the ground at the right moment, which they *usually* did.)

The curries came out, and the steam coming off Keith and David's plates caused Ginny's eyes to water and sting. David poked at his and listened to Keith talk with a dull, unchanging expression. His phone rang. He looked at the number and his eyes widened.

"Don't," Keith said, stabbing at David's cell phone with his curry-stained fork.

David looked pained.

"Have to," he said, snatching it up. "Be right back."

"So," Keith said when David had gone. "Let's review. Last night you mysteriously give me one hundred and forty-two pounds and then run out. And tonight you show up in front of my house as my flatmate suffers an emotional collapse. I was just wondering what it all means."

Before she could answer, the waiter sprang at his chance to brush some crumbs from David's chair. He had been hanging around their table like a vulture, waiting for them to eat the last papadam crumb so he could take away the basket. He eyed the last piece sadly, as if it was the barrier between him and eternal happiness. Ginny grabbed it and shoved it in her mouth. The man looked relieved and took the basket but immediately returned to stare mournfully at their water glasses. And then David came back in and dropped heavily into his chair. The waiter immediately pounced on him, offering another beer. He nodded tiredly. Keith turned his glance from Ginny to David.

"Well?"

"Just some stuff she wants back," he said.

Nothing was said until the waiter came back a moment later with another enormous bottle of beer. David tipped it back and chugged in several large gulping motions, drinking a good third of it in one go.

The phone call and the beer loosened David. He was usually polite, but now he was morphing into someone else. He launched into a list of all the things that he had long despised

98

about Fiona and that he had apparently noticed but kept inside.

And of course he would have another beer.

At first, this catharsis seemed good. David seemed to be coming back to reality. But then he began leering at a woman at another table who was clearly annoyed that he was talking too loudly. He chomped away at his curry and became louder and louder.

"He's guttered," Keith said. "Time to go."

Keith asked the ever-available waiter for the bill and threw down some crumpled bills. They seemed to be the same ones she had just given him the night before. She could practically recognize her own grip marks.

"I'll go get the car," he said. "Stay here with him, all right?"

David looked around and, seeing that Keith was gone, got up and stumbled for the door. Ginny followed him. David was waiting on the sidewalk, looking down the street as if lost.

Ginny hung nervously by the door.

"People don't change," he said. "You just sort of have to take them like they are. Know what I mean?"

"I guess," Ginny said uncertainly.

"Could you go and get me an ice cream?" he asked, nodding at a shop next to them with a large ice cream display. "I want an ice cream."

Getting up had caused David to lose a lot of steam. Besides, ice cream at a time like this was something she could understand. She went into the shop and picked out a rich-looking chocolate-covered bar. When she came back outside, however, he was gone.

She was still standing there, holding the rapidly melting ice cream, when Keith pulled up.

"He did a runner?" he asked.

Ginny nodded.

"I'll drive this way," he said. "You check the other way. Meet me back right here."

There were an amazing number of people on Brick Lane that night, mostly groups of guys in suits. She spotted David a few stores up, staring at the menu for another restaurant. When he saw Ginny, he started running again, and Ginny had no choice but to go right after him. Excessive alcohol apparently brought out the evil imp in David. Whenever Ginny would fall behind, he would stop and stand there, grinning. When she was close enough to see his smile, he would start off again.

To her relief, Keith's car turned the corner. Keith was almost on him when David turned and ran back the other way, toward Ginny. There was no way for Keith to turn around, so he had to keep going. It was up to Ginny to keep after him.

David led her all around the area, through residential streets, through streets with closed-up sari and cloth shops. They went deeper and deeper into less welcoming streets. She was breathing hard, and the curry was killing her stomach, but she stayed on him. After about ten minutes, she accepted the fact that David wasn't going to give up the game. She was going to have to play dirty. She let out a scream, then collapsed to the sidewalk, clutching at her leg. David turned again, but this time, even in his haze, he knew something was wrong. He hesitated but, seeing that Ginny was going no farther, stayed where he was.

He didn't even see Keith run up behind him and tackle him. He pressed David to the sidewalk and sat on his back.

"Very nice with the leg," Keith said, heaving for breath. "Cor . . . who knew he could run?"

Within a few moments of being held still, David slipped into a passive, near-unconscious state. Keith pulled him up and walked him to the car. Ginny scrambled into the backseat so that David could be carefully set in the front.

"He's going to honk in my car," Keith said sadly as they pulled away. "And I just cleaned it."

Ginny looked around at the collection of bags and garbage around her on the tiny backseat.

"You did?"

"Well, I put all that stuff back there."

Ginny reached up and shifted a rapidly sliding David into an upright position.

"I'm taking him to my place. Let him sleep it off there. I'll keep an eye on him. I'll take you home."

David made it to the sidewalk in front of Richard's house before Keith's prediction came to pass. As soon as they stopped, he opened the door and unleashed his worst. When he had recovered, Keith and Ginny walked him up and down the street a few times until the spell seemed over, then brought him back and leaned him against the gate.

"He'll be all right," Keith said, nodding. "He needed that. Clears the head."

David was slowly slipping down the gate. Keith grabbed him by the arm and propped him back up.

"Better go," he said. "That was good, what you did with your leg. Very good. Fast, too. You're not totally mad."

"Um . . ."

"Yes?"

"Earlier . . ."

"Yes?"

"I was coming to ask you if you wanted to go to Scotland with me," she said quickly. "I have to go to Edinburgh, and since you said . . ."

"What are you going there for?"

"I'm just . . . going."

"When?"

"Tomorrow?"

David lunged forward and fell against the hood of Keith's car. Keith stepped over. It looked like he was reaching for David, but at the last moment, he turned, took Ginny's face in his hands, and kissed her. It wasn't a tender, slow, "your lips are like delicate flower petals" kiss. More like a "thank-you" kiss. Or even a "good game!" kiss.

"Might as well," he said. "Show's not until ten tomorrow night. Kings Cross Station. Tomorrow morning. Eight thirty. In front of Virgin Rail."

Before she could even react, Keith had grabbed David and stuffed him into the car; he gave her a quick salute before driving away. Ginny stood there for several minutes, unable to move. She put her fingers lightly on her mouth, as if to hold the sensation there.

She didn't even notice right away that a small animal had come out from behind a nearby car and was slowly making its way toward the trash can she was standing near. She flipped through some old files in her mind, trying to come up with what this thing might be, and after a few seconds decided that— impossible as it seemed—it was a fox. She had only ever seen foxes in illustrations in a book of collected fairy tales. This thing looked like those pictures: it had a long snout, a small nose, red fur, and a shy, thief-like gait. It pawed closer to her, tilting its head curiously, as if asking her if she had plans on going through that trash can first.

"No," she said aloud, and then immediately wondered why she was talking to what was probably a fox—a fox that could very well be rabid and preparing to leap for her throat. Strangely, she had no fear.

The fox seemed to understand her answer and gracefully jumped up to the rim of the trash and dropped down inside. The big plastic bin rattled as he explored its contents. Ginny felt herself filled with a weird, swelling affection for the fox. It had seen her kiss. It was unafraid of her. It was hunting. It was hungry.

"Hope you find something good," she said quietly, then turned to go inside.

The Master and the Hairdresser

The ride to Scotland took four and a half hours, most of which Keith spent dead asleep with his head against the window, a comic book ("it's a *graphic monthly*") clutched in the grip of his fingerless leather gloves. He woke with a snort and jerk of the head just as the train was pulling into Edinburgh.

"Waverly Station?" he asked, blinking slowly. "Right. Out, or we'll end up in Aberdeen."

They came out of the station (which looked pretty much like the station they'd just left) and walked up a long flight of steps to street level. They were on a street full of large department stores. But unlike London, which felt low and compact and overstuffed, Edinburgh felt wide and open. The sky stretched wide and blue above them, and when Ginny turned around, she saw that the city seemed to be on a hundred different levels. It scooped and dipped. Over to her right, sitting high on a great jutting piece of rock like a pedestal, was a castle.

Keith took a deep breath and banged on his chest.

"All right," he said. "Who's this you've got to go see?"

"A friend of my aunt's. Some painter. I have a map to her house. . . ."

"Let's have a look."

He took the letter out of Ginny's hands before she could say a word.

"Mari Adams?" he asked. "I know this name."

"She's supposed to be kind of famous," Ginny said, almost as an apology.

"Oh." He studied the directions some more and frowned. "She lives in Leith, on the other side of the city. Right. You'll never find this. We'd better go together. Let me just stop into the Fringe office, and then we'll go."

"You don't have to . . ."

"I'm telling you, you *will* get lost. And I can't have that. Come on."

He was right. There was no way she could have found her way to Mari's on her own. Keith could barely work out the bus map to get to her corner of the city, and it took both of them to puzzle out the exact location of her house. She lived along a large body of water that Keith identified as being something called the Firth of Forth.

Since they were so far from where they started, Keith couldn't just turn around and go back, so he took it upon himself to come along with Ginny right up to Mari's door. There was an intricate pattern painted all around the door frame—gold salamanders, a fox, birds, flowers. The door knocker was a giant woman's head with a large nose ring. Ginny banged this once, then retreated down a few steps.

A moment later, a girl swung open the door. She wore red denim overalls with magnetic toy alphabet pieces sewn onto them with thick, obvious stitches. Also, she wore no shirt—she'd just clipped the overalls up as high as they could go. Her scowling face was crowned by a head of hair that had been bleached to a crisp white. It was short and jagged on top and long and braided in the back—a mullet-dread crossbreed.

"Yeah?" she said.

"Um . . . hi."

"Yeah."

It was going well so far.

"My aunt stayed here," Ginny said, trying not to stare at any one aspect of the girl's appearance for too long. "Her name was Peg? Margaret? Margaret Bannister?"

An unresponsive stare. Ginny noticed that the girl's eyebrows were almost as deeply chocolate brown as her own.

"I'm supposed to come here," Ginny said, waving around the blue envelope as if it were a visa allowing her access to the houses of total strangers. One of the strong summer winds came along and snapped the thin paper around, almost taking it from Ginny's hand.

"Yeah, all right." The girl had a hard Scottish brogue. "Hold on."

She shut the door in their faces.

"Friendly," Keith said. "You have to give her that."

"Would you shut up?" Ginny heard herself saying.

"Feisty."

"I'm nervous."

"Can't see why," he said, innocently examining the drawings around the door. "Seems perfectly normal."

Five minutes later, the door opened again.

"Mari's working," she said. "But she says you're tae come in."

The girl left the door hanging open, which they took as a sign that they were supposed to follow.

They were in a very old house, certainly. There were large fireplaces in each of the rooms with little piles of ash sitting under the grates. There was the lingering hint of burned wood in the air, even though Ginny suspected that the ashes were weeks old. The floors were all bare, with the occasionally furry white rug tossed here and there, with no apparent logic. Every room was painted differently: powder blue in one room, maroon in the next, bright spring onion green in the hall. The windowsills and edging around the floor were all egg-yolk yellow. The only piece of furniture in the first few rooms was a massive, ornate cherrywood table with a marble top and a big mirror. It was covered in little toys: chattering teeth, tops, little cars, a boxing nun puppet, and a windup Godzilla.

But everywhere—everywhere—there were paintings. Massive paintings of women, mostly. Women with sprawling masses of hair with all kinds of things coming out of it, women juggling stars. Floating women, women sneaking through black forests, women surrounded by bright shimmering gold. Paintings so large that the walls could each only accommodate one or two.

The girl continued to lead them back, then up three flights along a rickety wooden staircase that was lined with even more paintings. At the top, they reached a doorway that had been painted a bright metallic gold.

"Here," the girl said, turning and heading back downstairs.

Ginny and Keith stared at the big gold door.

"Who are we visiting again?" he asked. "God?"

In answer, the door swung open.

Ginny wouldn't have guessed that the girl at the door could have lost the "Unusual and Imposing Appearance Award" so quickly, but Mari beat her by a mile. She had to be sixty, at least. Ginny could see it in her face. She had a massive crown of long, teased-out jet black hair cut through with orange highlights. She was wearing clothes that were just a bit too small and tight for her plump frame—a vertical-striped boatneck shirt and jeans with a black belt covered in heavy studs. It gripped her belly unflatteringly, yet somehow she carried it off. Her eyes were completely surrounded by heavy circles of black eyeliner. There were what looked like three identical freckles along each of her cheekbones, right under her eyes. As Ginny stepped into the room, she could see that they were small blue tattoos of stars. She wore flat gold sandals, and Ginny could see that there were also tattoos on her feet, words printed in tiny purple scrawl. When she reached out to clasp Ginny by the face and give her a kiss on each cheek, Ginny saw similar messages on her hands.

"You're Peg's niece?" Mari asked, breaking the embrace.

Ginny nodded.

"And you are?" This was to Keith.

"Her hairdresser," he said. "She won't go anywhere without me."

Mari patted his cheek and smiled.

"I like you," she said. "Would you like a chocolate?"

She padded over to her sunny worktable and produced a large bucket of miniature candy bars. Ginny shook her head, but Keith took a small handful.

"I'll get Chloe to bring us some tea," she said.

A few minutes later, Chloe (maybe the last name in the world Ginny would have attached to the red overalls girl—she was more of a "Hank") came up with a ceramic tray with a brown teapot, a dish of sugar, and a small jug of cream. The tray was also littered with even more miniature chocolate bars. As Mari reached for these, she noticed that Keith's gaze was lingering on the words imprinted on her hands.

"These are the names of my dogs, the ones that have died," Mari said. "I've dedicated my hands to them. My foxes' names are on my feet."

Instead of the logical, "You had foxes? And you put their names on your FEET?" Ginny managed to say, "I think I saw a fox. Last night. In London."

"You probably did," Mari said. "London is full of foxes. It's a magical city. I had three pet foxes. When I lived in France, I had a cage built in the garden. I locked myself in there with them during the days and painted. Foxes are wonderful companions."

Keith looked like he was about to say something, but Ginny planted her foot firmly on the toe of his Chucks and pressed down.

"It's good to be in a cage," Mari went on. "It keeps you focused. I recommend it."

Ginny ground her foot down hard. Keith pressed his lips together tightly and turned to look at the paintings on the wall just next to him. Mari poured out the tea and loaded her cup with sugar, stirring it loudly.

"I'm so sorry about your aunt," she finally said. "It was such terrible news to hear that she died. But she was so ill . . ."

Keith turned from a painting of a woman morphing into a can of beans and raised an eyebrow in Ginny's direction.

"She mentioned you might be coming. I'm glad you did. She was a very good painter, you know. Very good."

"She left me some letters," Ginny said, avoiding Keith's gaze. "She asked me to come here, to see you."

"She mentioned that she had a niece." Mari nodded knowingly. "She felt so bad for leaving you behind."

Keith's eyebrow went up higher.

"I lived without a home for a long time," she went on. "I lived on the streets in Paris. No money. Just my paints in a bag, one spare dress, and a big furry coat I wore all year long. I used to run past outdoor cafés and steal food off people's plates. I'd sit under the bridges in the summertime and paint for a whole day straight. I was crazy then, but it was just something I had to do."

Ginny felt her throat go dry and had the uneasy feeling that both Keith and Mari were watching her closely. It didn't help that she was sitting in a spot of sunlight coming in through the ancient multi-paneled window above Mari's worktable. Mari thoughtfully pushed one of her little chocolate wrappers around the table with her finger.

"Come," she said. "I'll show you something. Both of you."

At the back of the room, in what looked like a closet, was the narrowest set of stairs Ginny had ever encountered. They were made of stone and spiraled tightly. Mari's body could just about squeeze through. They emerged in an attic, which had a low, curved ceiling painted a bright, cotton candy pink. The room smelled like burned toast and several centuries of dust, and it was filled with shelves loaded down with massive art books, with spines featuring titles in every language Ginny could recognize and lots more that she couldn't.

Mari pulled down a particularly large book that had a thick crust of dust along the top and banged it open on one of the tables. She flipped through the pages for a moment until she came to the print she wanted. It was a very old, intensely colored image of a man and woman holding hands. It was an incredibly precise picture, almost as clear as a photograph.

"This is by Jan van Eyck," she said, poking at the picture. "It's a painting of an engagement. It's an ordinary scene—there are shoes on the floor, a dog. He's recording the event. Just two ordinary people getting engaged. No one had ever gone to so much effort to record ordinary people before."

Ginny realized that Keith hadn't tried to make a comment for a while. He was looking at the picture intently.

"Here," Mari said, pointing a long emerald green fingernail at the center of the picture. "Right here in the middle. The focal point. You see what's there? It's a mirror. And in the reflection, that's the artist. He painted himself into the picture. And right above it is an inscription. It says, 'Jan van Eyck was here.'"

She closed the book shut as punctuation, and a dust bunny puffed into the air.

"Sometimes artists like to catch themselves looking out, let the world see them for once. It's a signature. This one is a very bold one. But this is also a witnessing. We want to remember, and we want to be remembered. That's why we paint."

Mari was just getting to something that seemed like a clear message—something Ginny could wrap her head around. *We want to remember, and we want to be remembered. That's why we paint.*

But then Mari went on.

"I marked my hands and feet to remember my companions, the ones I loved," she said, looking at her tattoos.

Keith's eyes lit up and he got as far as opening his mouth and making an "eeee" sound before Ginny got to his foot again.

"What's your birthday?" Mari asked.

"August eighteenth," Ginny replied, confused.

"Leo. Ah. Back downstairs, love."

They oozed back down the stone steps. There was no rail, so Ginny gripped the wall for support. Mari shuffled back to her worktable and patted a stool next to it, indicating that Ginny should sit. Ginny crossed over uncertainly.

"Right. Let's see." She eyed Ginny up and down. "Why don't you just take off your shirt, then?"

Keith folded his arms and sat on the floor in the corner, deliberately not averting his eyes. Ginny turned her back to him and self-consciously pulled off her shirt, wishing she'd put on a nicer bra. She had packed a good one, but of course she'd put on the stretchy, sporty gray one.

"Yes," Mari said, examining Ginny's skin. "I think the shoulder. Your aunt was an Aquarius. It makes so much sense, when you think about it. Stay still now."

Mari picked up her pens and began to draw.

Ginny could feel the pen strokes on the back of her shoulder. They didn't hurt, but there was a sharpness to the pen. It didn't seem right to complain; after all, there was a famous artist drawing on her. Not that she knew why.

Mari was a slow worker, drawing dot by dot, poke by poke, working against the pull of the skin. She got up frequently for chocolate, or to look at a bird that had come to the feeder in the window, or to stare at Ginny from the front. It took so long that Keith fell asleep in the corner and began to snore.

"There," Mari said, sitting back and looking over her work. "It won't last forever. It will fade. But that's how it should be this time, don't you think, love? Unless you'd like it tattooed in. I know a very good place."

She pulled a tiny mirror out from a drawer of supplies and tried to hold it at an angle that Ginny could see. She had to crane her neck around painfully, but she caught a glimpse of it. It was a lion, colored in bright gold. His mane shot out wildly in all directions (big hair seemed to be a theme with Mari), eventually turning into shooting blue rivulets.

"You're both welcome to stay," Mari said. "I'll have Chloe—"

"The train," Keith said quickly. "We have to catch the train."

"We have to catch the train," Ginny repeated. "But thanks. For everything."

Mari walked them to the door, and on the top step she stepped forward and wrapped her fleshy arms around Ginny. Her crazy hair filled Ginny's field of vision, and the world was black with streaks of orange.

"Keep this one," she whispered into Ginny's ear. "I like him."

She stepped back, winked at Keith, and then closed the door. They both blinked at the patterns of salamanders for a moment.

"So," Keith said, taking Ginny by the arm and leading her back in the direction of the bus, "now that we've met with Lady MacStrange, why don't you explain to me what's been going on?"

114

The Monsters Attack

Outside the train on the ride home, the scenery was changing rapidly. First city, then green hills and pastures with hundreds of sheep nibbling at endless patches of green grass. Then they were riding along the sea, and then through towns with tiny brick houses and looming, unbelievable churches. There was strong sun, sudden fog, then a final bright burst of purple as it slowly got dark. The passing English towns were just streaks of orange streetlights.

It had taken almost the entire ride to explain the basics. She'd had to go back to the very beginning of everything . . . back to New York, back to Aunt Peg's "today I live in" games. She brushed quickly over the events of the last few months—the phone call from Richard, the horrible sinking feeling, the drive up to the airport to claim the body—and got to the interesting part, the arrival of the package with the envelopes. She waited for Keith's big reaction, but all she got was:

"That's a bit crap, isn't it?"

"What?"

"The artist excuse. If you can call that an excuse."

"You really had to know her," she said, trying hard to make it sound light.

"No, I don't. That is crap. I know crap. I have seen crap before. The more you tell me about your aunt, the less I like her."

Ginny felt her eyes narrowing a little.

"You didn't know her," she said.

"You've told me enough. I don't like what she did to you. She seems to have meant the world to you when you were a kid, and she just left one day without a word. And her entire explanation to you comes in the form of a few very odd little envelopes."

"No," she said, feeling an anger rising suddenly. "Everything interesting that ever happened to me happened because of her. Without her, I'm boring. You don't get it because *you* have stories."

"Everyone has stories," he said dismissively.

"Not good ones, like yours. They aren't as interesting. You got *arrested*. I couldn't have gotten arrested if I tried."

"It doesn't take a lot of effort," he said. "Besides, it wasn't getting arrested that was the problem."

"Problem?"

He drummed his fingers on the table, then turned and looked at her for a moment.

"Okay," he said. "You told your story, might as well tell you mine while we're here. When I was sixteen, I had a girlfriend. Her name was Claire. I was worse than David. She was all I thought about. Didn't care about school, didn't care about anything. I stopped mucking about because I was spending all my time with her."

"Why is that a problem?"

"Well, she got pregnant," he said, flicking the edge of the table with his finger. "And that was a bit of a mess."

It was one thing to know Keith had had sex. That should have been obvious since he was Keith, and not her, not so painfully virginal. But *pregnancy* was a step beyond anything she could really process. That implied a lot of sex. So much sex. So much that he could say it all casually.

Ginny looked down at the table. Obviously, she knew these things happened, but they never happened to her or to her friends. They happened on TV or to people in school who she didn't know. Somehow, those kinds of stories always trickled down to the general populace months after they happened, giving the people involved a permanent, shiny veneer of maturity that she would never, ever have. She couldn't even drive after ten o'clock at night.

"Are you horrified?" he asked, glancing over. "It does happen, you know."

"I know," she said quickly. "What happened? I mean, did she—?"

She caught herself short. What was she saying?

"I'm not a dad, if that's what you're asking," he said.

Well, yes. That was *exactly* what she was so cleverly asking. This was why nothing ever happened to her. She couldn't handle the excitement. She couldn't even make it through a conversation about something serious and sexual without blowing it.

"It's a fair question," he said. "I offered to leave school and get a job. I was ready to do it, too. But she didn't want to leave school, so she decided there was only one thing she could do about it. I can't blame her."

They rode in silence for a few minutes, both rocking slightly in time with the train and staring at the poster for the train's "Get some food!" promotion, which featured a picture of a bald man who was the "pork king of the north."

"The problem," he finally said, "was that things were never right after that. I kept trying to make it better, to talk to her, but she didn't want to talk to me about it. She just wanted to get on with her life. So she did. It took me months to get the hint. I was a mess. But now everything's sorted."

He smiled brightly and folded his hands on the table.

"What do you mean?"

"I mean, once you go through something like that, you learn. Went on a bit of a bender after that. Stole a car—just took it around for a few hours, don't know why. Wasn't even that nice. Then woke up one morning, realized that I had to take my exams and that my life was still going on. I got myself together, got into school. Now I am the rabid success that you see before you today. Just want to make my plays. That's all I need. And see how it's worked out? That's how I met you, isn't it?"

He threw his arm around her shoulders and gave her a friendly shake. Again, it wasn't overly romantic. This gesture had a "good dog!" feel to it. But there was something else, too. Something that said, "I'm not just here because you give me big handfuls of cash for no reason. Things are different now." Maybe it was the fact that he kept his arm there for the rest of the trip home and neither of them felt the need to say another word.

Half an hour later, they were standing on the platform at Kings Cross, waiting for the tube.

"Almost forgot," he said, reaching into the pocket of his jacket. "I have something for you."

He produced a small windup Godzilla, which looked exactly like the one from Mari's house.

"Is that from Mari's?" she asked.

"Yep."

"You *stole* it?"

"I couldn't help it," he said, smiling. "You needed a souvenir."

"Why did you think I'd want something that was stolen?" Ginny felt herself stepping back, away from him.

Keith stepped back a bit and lost his grin.

"Wait a minute. . . ."

"Maybe it was part of some art piece!"

"A major work ruined."

"It doesn't matter," Ginny said. "It was hers. It's from her house."

"I'll write her a letter and give myself up," he said, holding up his hands. "I took the Godzilla. Call off the search. It was me, but I blame society."

"It's not funny."

"I nicked a little toy," he said, pinching the Godzilla between his fingers. "It's nothing."

"It's not nothing."

"Fine." Keith walked over to the edge of the platform and

tossed the little toy down onto the tracks, then wandered back.

"What did you do that for?" Ginny asked.

"You didn't want it."

"That doesn't mean you should just get rid of it," she said.

"Sorry. Was I supposed to take it back?"

"You weren't supposed to take it in the first place!"

"Know what I'll take?" he asked. "The bus. See you."

He disappeared through the crowd before Ginny could even manage to turn around to watch him go.

#5
&
6

Dearest Ginger,

When I was a kid, I had an illustrated book of Roman mythology. I was completely obsessed with this book. My favorite of all the gods and goddesses, believe it or not, was Vesta, goddess of hearth and home.

I know. So unlikely. I mean, I've never owned a vacuum cleaner. But it's true. Out of all of the goddesses, she was the one I liked the most. Lots of hot young gods pursued her, but she made a vow of perpetual virginity. Her symbol, her home, was the fireplace. She was basically the goddess of central heating.

Vesta was worshiped in every town and in every home through fire. She was everywhere, and people depended on her every day. There was a large temple built in her honor in Rome, and priestesses at her temple were called the vestal virgins.

Being a vestal was a pretty sweet job. They had one major task: They had to make sure that the undying fire in Vesta's ceremonial hearth never went out. There were always six of them, so they could work in shifts. In exchange for this service, they were treated as divinities. They were given a palace to live in and had the same privileges as men. In times of crisis, they were called upon to give advice on matters of Roman national security. They got great tickets to the theater, people held parties for them, and they were paraded and revered everywhere.

The only catch? Try thirty years of celibacy. Thirty years of living with their fellow vestals, poking the fire and doing crossword puzzles. If they broke the virginity rule, they were taken to a place that translates as "Evil Fields" and led down a set of stairs to a small underground room with a bed and a lamp. Once they were in, the door to the room was shut, the steps pulled up, and the whole thing sealed over in dirt. Which is pretty harsh.

Still, you've got to hand it to the vestal virgins. It may seem sad and scary--but realize just how much power people have always seen in women on their own.

The remains of their temple are in the Roman Forum, and you can see their statues. (The Forum is basically attached to the Colosseum.) Go and visit them, and make them an offering. This is your task. When you are done, you can open the next envelope, right there, in the temple.

As for where to stay, may I recommend a little place I stumbled on when I arrived in Rome? It's

not a hotel or a hostel--it's a private house with
one room for rent. It's run by a woman named
Ortensia. Her house isn't far from the main train
station. The address is on the back of this letter.

Va-va-voom,
Your Runaway Aunt

The Road to Rome

Ginny hated her backpack. It kept falling over on the scale because it was so weird and lumpy and tumor-like. It was more purple and green than ever in the fluorescent light of the airline counter. And it was obvious that the millions of straps (which she wasn't really sure she had laced right, so the entire thing could come apart at any second) were going to catch on the conveyor belt and stop it and all of the luggage would get backed up. Then the flight would be delayed, which would throw off the entire airport schedule and disrupt events in several countries.

Also, the nasally BudgetAir check-in woman had taken a little too much delight in telling Ginny, "Five kilos overweight. That'll be forty pounds." She was clearly unhappy when Ginny yanked on some of the straps and managed to get one of the pouches off, making the bag just the right weight.

As Ginny walked away from the check-in, she realized that this flight could not be safe if five kilograms made that much of a difference. This flight had also been purchased online that morning for the insane sum of £35. (It was called BudgetAir for a reason.)

Richard was standing by a slowly rotating display for duty-free liquor, wearing the same slightly baffled expression he'd worn when they'd met days earlier.

"I guess I should go," she said. "But thanks. For everything."

"I feel like you just got here," he replied, "like we didn't even get a chance to talk."

"I guess we didn't."

"No."

They began nodding at each other again, and then Richard swooped forward and gave her a hug.

"If you need anything—anything—don't hesitate to call. You know where to find me."

"I know," she said.

There was nothing else to say, so Ginny carefully backed into the crowd. Richard waited there until she turned and headed off to her gate and was still there watching when she checked with a glance back as she entered security.

For some reason, the sight made her very sad, so she turned around sharply and kept her back turned until she was sure that he was out of sight.

When BudgetAir said the plane would land in Rome, they weren't being literal. What they meant to say was, "The plane will land in Italy; that much we will guarantee. The rest is up to you." Ginny found herself in a small airport that clearly wasn't Rome's main hub. There were a few small airlines represented, and most of the passengers getting off had "where the hell am I?" looks on their faces as they wandered the terminal.

She followed a trail of lost people headed out the door into the balmy evening. They stood on the sidewalk, heads swiveling back and forth. Finally, a flat-fronted, very European-looking bus pulled up with a sign that said ROMA TERMINI, and everyone got on. The driver said something to her in Italian, and when she didn't respond, he held up ten fingers. She gave him ten euros. This proved to be a good guess, and he gave her a ticket and let her pass.

Ginny had no idea a big square bus could go so fast. They rocketed along a highway and several smaller, curving roads. It was very dark, with occasional houses and gas stations. They were cresting a hill now, and below them Ginny could see a warm bright glow hanging in the air. They had to be coming into the city.

As they entered Rome, the bus was moving quickly enough to make everything a wondrous streak. The buildings were colorful, lit by multicolored lights. There were cobbled streets and hundreds of cafés. She caught a glimpse of a magnificent, massive fountain that hardly seemed like it could be real—it was built into the front of a palatial building and was composed of enormous sculptures of godlike human figures. Then there was a building right out of her history textbook chapter on ancient Rome—tall pillars, domed roof. It could have had people in togas standing on its steps. She started to feel a bubbling excitement. London had been amazing, but this was something totally different. This was travel. This was *foreign* and *old* and *cultural*.

Another sharp turn took them down a massive boulevard,

and the buildings became more practical and industrial. They came to an abrupt stop in front of a massive glass-and-metal box of a building. The driver opened the door and sat back and said nothing. People peeled themselves from their seats and pulled their luggage off the rack. Ginny suited up with the pack and lumbered out.

She managed to wave down a taxi (at least she thought that was what it was, and it stopped) and passed the letter forward, showing the driver the address. A few minutes later, after cheating death by speeding down roads just barely wide enough to fit the car, they pulled up in front of a small green house. Three cats groomed each other on the front step, oblivious to the squealing machine that had just arrived in front of them.

The woman who opened the door looked about fifty years old. She had short black hair, streaked elegantly with gray. She was carefully but not overly made up, and she was dressed in an attractive blouse and skirt. She wore heels. She ushered Ginny inside. This had to be Ortensia.

"Hello," Ginny said.

"Hello," the woman replied.

She had a nervous look in her eye that said: "That is all the English I know. Go no further because all I will do is stare at you."

The backpack, though, could be universally understood. The woman pulled out a small preprinted card that said 20 EUROS PER NIGHT in English as well as some other languages, and Ginny nodded and passed over the money.

Ortensia led her to a tiny room two flights up. It looked like it was originally a crawl space, since there was just enough headroom for her to stand and just about enough room for the cot-bed, a small dresser, and her backpack. A realtor would have described it as "charming." It *was* kind of charming, actually. It had been painted a happy mint green (not a sad, cinder-block–gym-wall mint green). Plants filled every available space. It would have been very nice in the winter, but now it was the holding tank for all the rising heat. Ortensia pushed open the window, and a lazy breeze came in, circulated once, and went home.

Ortensia said a few words in Italian that Ginny was pretty sure meant good night, then descended the narrow spiral stairs that led to the room. Ginny sat on her neatly made bed. It was quiet in her little room. It made her heart pound. She suddenly felt very, very alone. She told herself to stop thinking about it, changed for bed, and lay awake, listening to the Roman traffic out on the street.

Virginia and the Virgins

Every once in a while, Ginny remembered that along with being charming and whimsical, Aunt Peg could sometimes be a little flaky. She was the kind of person who absentmindedly stirred her coffee with her pinkie and was surprised when she burned herself or left the car in neutral instead of park and laughed when it was occasionally in a different place than where she had left it. Those things had always been funny before. But now, with the massive, ancient city of Rome sprawled out around her and absolutely no guide, Ginny had to wonder how good (or funny) the "no map" rule really was. Her sense of direction wasn't going to help her much here—there was just too much Rome and no point of reference to work from. It was all crumbling walls and huge billboards and wide squares and statues.

On top of that, she was terrified of crossing the street, since everyone drove like a stunt extra from a movie car chase. (Even the nuns, of which there were plenty.) Ginny confined herself to one side of a road and crossed intersections only with groups of more than twenty.

And it was hot. So much hotter than London. It was real summer here.

After an hour of wandering around what seemed like the same tight streets of pharmacies and video rental stores, she spotted a tour group walking along with flags and matching travel bags. Lacking any other plan, she decided to trail them loosely in the hopes that they'd be going somewhere big and touristy. Then at least she'd be *somewhere*.

As she walked, she noticed a few things. The tourists wore sandals or sneakers and carried heavy bags or maps. They looked hot, and they guzzled bottles of water or soda. She even saw a few people buzzing themselves with tiny, battery-powered handheld fans. They looked ridiculous, but Ginny knew she wasn't doing much better. Her bag was stuck to her back. Her braids were limp in the heat. The little makeup she wore had dribbled off her face. She was developing a nasty sweat pocket at the middle of her bra that was going to start showing through her shirt at any second. And her sneakers were squeakier than usual.

The Roman women flew past on Vespa scooters with their designer handbags resting by their feet. They wore huge, fabulous sunglasses. They smoked. Talked on their cell phones. Threw dramatic glances over their shoulders at people who passed them by. Most amazingly, they did it all *in heels,* gracefully, without teetering over on the cobblestones or getting stuck in a crack on the uneven pavements. They didn't break down and cry from the blisters that had to be forming as the sweltering heat caused the leather of their stilettos to suction to their perfectly pedicured feet.

They were hard for Ginny to watch. They made her nervous.

She followed a group down into a metro station and lost them as she struggled to buy her tickets. She went over to a map and found, to her relief, that there was a stop marked Coliseo, with a drawing that looked a lot like a doughnut. When she emerged again into the blinding Roman sunlight, she was on a busy road. It seemed certain that she had made a mistake until she turned and found that the Colosseum was directly behind her. It took her a few minutes to make it across the street.

Again, she met another tour group, and she trailed along behind, following them under one of the massive archways that led inside. The guide seemed to take a little too much pleasure in reporting the bloodshed that had made the Colosseum so popular back in the day.

". . . and at the inaugural, over five thousand animals were slaughtered!"

A woman in a long, double-sided apron was walking toward them. She opened a large bag she was carrying. Within a moment, a flurry of cats appeared around them. They seemed to leak from the walls. They jumped from hidden ledges high up in the stony walls. They rushed from behind Ginny and gathered together in a tangle, mewing loudly. The woman smiled and began pulling paper takeout containers full of bright red raw meat and pasta. She set these down on the ground, allowing a few feet between each dish, and the cats swarmed around. Ginny could actually hear them frantically chewing the food and purring loudly. When they were finished eating a few moments later, they surrounded the woman, rubbing hard against her ankles.

Ginny and the tour group crossed through a passageway into the Roman Forum. The Forum looked like a very old place that had been run through by a giant bowling ball. Some columns, though cracked and worn, were still standing. Others were just little nubs in the ground, strange little stone tree stumps. Ancient buildings sat on the rocky outlines of other, even more ancient but now-missing buildings. The group split up to explore. Ginny decided to ask the guide where to go—he didn't seem that aware of who was with him.

"I'm looking for the vestal virgins," Ginny said. "Their temple is supposed to be in here."

"The virgins!" he said, raising his hands in delight. "You come with me."

They made their way through the labyrinth of walls and paths and columns to two rectangular pools made of stone, obviously ancient but refilled and planted around with flowers. On one side was a line of statues on tall square pedestals. All women, all wrapped in flowing Roman robes. Most of them were missing their heads. Some, most of their bodies. Eight figures stood, with a few empty pedestals between them. The other side was full of empty pedestals or just remnants of pedestals. The pedestals and statues were protected from the crowd by a low metal rail— nothing much, no more than a mild request not to touch.

"The virgins," he said proudly. "Lovely."

Ginny leaned into the rail and looked over the statues. She felt that weird guilt she sometimes got when she knew she was looking at something very old and important and she just didn't . . . get it. The story behind them was interesting, but they were still just a bunch of broken statues.

Come to think of it . . . it was a little annoying that Aunt Peg had sent her to look at a bunch of famous virgins. What exactly was that supposed to mean?

For some reason, this made her think of Keith. That memory stung. She pulled off her daypack very deliberately and dug around inside. She had a few euros and euro coins. A gum wrapper. The key to her room at Ortensia's. The next letter. Her eye patch thing from the plane. Nothing that seemed like an appropriate gift to give a bunch of ancient statues. This whole thing was suddenly very annoying. It was too hot. The symbolism was a little too pointed. This entire exercise was stupid.

She finally found an American quarter at the bottom of the bag. It seemed as good an offering as any. She lobbed it softly onto the grass between two of the statues, then pulled out the next letter. It was painted all over with pictures of tiny cakes.

"Okay," she said, tearing open the seal. "What now?"

6

Dear Virginia,

Sorry. If there was ever a moment to use your proper name, this seemed like it. (This is one of those things that isn't funny . . . isn't it?)

So here you are, standing around in a big courtyard of broken stuff, probably surrounded by tourists. (You are not a tourist . . . you are on a quest. You are a quest . . . ioner. Ooh. I should stop, huh?)

Anyway, what do we learn from this, Gin? What do our girls the vestals tell us?

Well, for a start, single chicks are powerful chicks. And in some situations, dating can be bad for you. However, since at least a handful of the vestals risked everything for a little loving, we also know that . . . sometimes, it just feels like it's worth it.

See, I had a problem, Gin. I was very into this idea of being a single woman, committed to a higher purpose, like the vestals. The way I saw it, the great artists didn't want to be comfortable. They wanted to struggle--alone--them against the world. So I wanted to struggle.

Whenever I got too comfortable anywhere, I felt like I had to move on. I did it with all kinds of things. I quit whenever I started liking a job too much. I broke up with guys whenever things got too serious. I left New York because I was just too content. I wasn't moving forward. I know that it must have been hard when I left without a word . . . but that's how I always did it. I would sneak off like a thief in the night, maybe because I knew there was something just a little bit wrong about what I was doing.

At the same time, I still have this thing about Vesta . . . this love of the home. Part of me wanted to embrace that. I love this idea of a goddess who guards the fire, blesses the house. I am a mass of contradictions.

One of her other symbols was bread, anything baked. Bread was life itself to the Romans. On Vesta's holiday, animals used to be decorated with garlands of cake. Garlands of cake! (Screw flowers. Can you imagine any garland better than a garland of cake? I can't.) So, let's take this idea and celebrate Vesta with some cake. But let's do it the proper Roman way.

I want you to ask a Roman boy out for cake. (Or girl, if that turns out to be your preference. But good luck with that--Roman women are tigresses.) For the sake of argument, I'm going to say boy because Roman boys are some of the most amusing creatures on earth. You are a beautiful girl, Gin, and a Roman boy will tell you that in his own special way.

Unless things have changed a lot, Gin, I am going to guess that this will be hard for you. You were always so shy. It bothered me because I was worried that people might not get to know the wonder that was and is my niece Virginia Blackstone! But fear not. The Romans will help you. If there was ever a city to learn how to ask a stranger out, this is it.

Get out there, tiger. Let them eat cake.

Love,
Your Bundle of Issues Aunt

Boys and Cake

This bordered on being a nightmare scenario. This was adding insult to injury.

She followed the tour group out of the Colosseum and meandered along with them for almost an hour, stewing over this latest command. *Go see old virgins! Now ask a strange boy out, you shy, retarded thing!*

She didn't want to ask a boy out. She *was* shy (thanks for bringing it up). Plus, the guy she liked was in London, and he thought she was crazy. Salt. Wound. Together at last.

The tour group stopped in a large square with a crowd in the middle, all gathered around a fountain, clearly very old, carved into the shape of a sinking boat. Some dipped their hands in and drank the water. The group suddenly dispersed, leaving Ginny to her own devices once again.

She was thirsty. Her every instinct told her that she shouldn't be drinking fountain water, especially really old fountain water, but lots of people were doing it. Plus, she really needed a drink. She took her empty bottle from her bag, found an opening along the edge, and tentatively reached out to the spray. She took a long sip and was rewarded with cold, fresh water—water that tasted very safe. She drained her bottle and filled it again.

When she turned around, three little kids were running at her. Strangely, one was holding a newspaper. They were all girls, and they were extremely beautiful, with long, very dark brown hair and bright green eyes. The tallest of the girls, who couldn't have been older than ten, came right up to Ginny and started flapping the newspaper at her, shaking the pages. In the next second, a tall, kind of thin guy with a huge book suddenly leapt up from where he was sitting and started running at her as well, yelling things in Italian. Ginny involuntarily took a step back and heard a little squeal. She felt her foot come into contact with a tinier foot and her daypack make contact with a small, helpless face. She realized that the little girls were all circling, sort of dancing around her, and any move she made might result in taking another one of them out with her feet or bag, so she froze and started apologizing, even though she realized that they probably would not understand a word she was saying.

The guy was almost to them now and was waving around his fat, hardback book like he was trying to cut a path through some unseen foliage. The small newspaper flappers were understandably alarmed by this larger book flapper and immediately streamed away from Ginny. The guy broke his run with a few final, stumbling steps, stopping right as he got up to Ginny. He nodded in satisfaction.

Ginny still hadn't moved. She stared at him, wide-eyed.

"They were about to steal from you," he said. His English was very clear but strongly flavored by an Italian accent.

"Those little girls?" she asked.

"Yes. Believe me. I see this all of the time. They are gypsies."

"Gypsies?"

"You are all right? Has anything been taken?"

Ginny reached around and felt her pack. To her alarm, she found the zipper partway open. She opened it up all the way and checked the contents. Strangely, she checked first to make sure the letter was still in there, and then she checked for her money. Both were there.

"No," she said.

"That's good." He nodded. "Okay. Good."

He went back to his spot at the edge of the fountain and sat down. Ginny stared at him. He didn't look Italian. He had golden brown hair, almost blond. His eyes were light colored and very narrow.

If there was ever a guy to buy cake for, it was a guy who had just kept her from being robbed, even if that meant defending her from small children by waving a textbook.

She walked up to him cautiously. He looked up from his book.

"I was wondering . . ." Ginny began. "Well, first, thanks. Do you want to . . ."

Do you want to was too strong a construction. It meant, "Do you want to do this with me?" She just had to offer the cake. Everyone likes cake.

"I mean . . ." she corrected herself, "would you like some cake?"

"Cake?" he repeated.

He blinked slowly. Maybe at Ginny, maybe at the sun. Maybe his eyes were tired. Then he looked down into the splashing waters of the fountain. Ginny looked into them as well. Anything to keep her eyes off him in this painful pause, during which he had to be trying to figure out a way of telling a weird American girl to leave him alone.

"Not cake," he finally replied. "But a coffee."

Coffee . . . cake . . . close enough. She had asked a guy, and the guy had said yes. This was nothing short of a miracle. She stopped herself just short of bouncing on her heels.

It was no problem finding a coffee bar. They were everywhere. The guy went up to the long marble counter and turned casually, ready to take Ginny's order and pass it to the stiff-aproned server.

"I usually get a latte," she said.

"You would like a glass of milk? No, you mean a caffè latte. Would you like to sit?"

She pulled out a few euros.

"It costs more if you sit," he explained. "It's ridiculous, but we are Italians."

It cost a lot more. Ginny had to pass over about ten dollars' worth of euros, and in return, they were presented with two very modest glass cups, each nestled in a tiny metal basket with a handle.

They sat down at one of the gray marble-topped tables, and the boy began to talk. His name was Beppe. He was twenty. He was a student, studying to be a teacher. He had three older sisters. He liked cars, some British bands Ginny hadn't heard of. He had been surfing in Greece. He didn't ask Ginny a lot about herself, something she could easily live with.

"It's hot," he said. "You should have a gelato. Have you had one yet?"

He was horrified to hear that she hadn't.

"Come on," he said, getting up. "We're going now. This is ridiculous."

Beppe led her down a few more streets, streets that got progressively more crowded with people and more colorful. These were streets that shouldn't have had motorcycles and scooters barreling down them but did anyway. People calmly stepped out of the way just inches from their deaths, sometimes offering a choice word or gesture if they'd actually been brushed.

Beppe finally stopped in front of a small, unassuming stoop. Once Ginny stepped inside, however, she saw that its size didn't reflect its offerings. There were dozens of colorful gelatos packed into a glass case. Two men behind the counter quickly shoveled out heroic portions with a flat-edged spoon. Beppe translated the labels. There were normal flavors like strawberry, chocolate. But there were also ginger and cinnamon, cream with wild honey, black licorice. One was rice flavored, and there were at least half a dozen with special liquors or wine.

"How did you come here?" he asked as she selected her flavor, which was the unimaginative strawberry.

"By . . . plane?"

"You are with a tour," he said, but not as a question. He seemed certain of this.

"No tour. Just me."

"You came to Rome by yourself? With no one? No friends?"

"Just me."

"My sister lives in Travestere," he suddenly said, giving Ginny a short nod, as if she should know what this meant.

"What's that?"

"Travestere? The best place in Rome," he said. "My sister will like you. You will like my sister. Get your ice cream, then we will go to see my sister."

Beppe's Sister

Travestere *couldn't* be a real place. It looked like Disney had attacked a corner of Rome with leftover pastel paint and created the coziest, most picturesque neighborhood ever. It seemed to consist entirely of nooks. There were shutters on the windows, overflowing window boxes, hand-lettered signs that were fading perfectly. There were wash lines hung from building to building, draped with white sheets and shirts. All around her were people with cameras, photographing the wash.

"I know," Beppe said, eyeing the photographers. "It's ridiculous. Where is your camera? You can take a picture too."

"I don't have one."

"Why don't you have a camera? All Americans bring cameras."

"I don't know," she lied. "I just didn't."

They walked on a little farther and finally stopped in front of an orange-colored flat-faced building with a slightly green-tinted roof. He pulled some keys from his pocket and opened up an ornate wooden door.

The inside of the building was nothing like the outside. In fact, it looked like Aunt Peg's old New York apartment building—chipped tile floor and dented metal mailboxes. She followed Beppe up three flights of stairs to a stifling, dark hallway. From there, he showed her into a very clean, somewhat spare apartment. It was just one room, carefully divided into sections with folding screens and furniture.

Beppe pushed open a large window above the kitchen table, and they had a good view of the street and the bedroom of the neighbor across the way. She was sprawled on her bed, reading a magazine. A fat fly came in through the unscreened window.

"Where's your sister?" Ginny asked, looking around the empty room.

"My sister is a doctor," he explained. "She is very busy, all the time. I am the student, the lazy one."

This wasn't exactly an answer, but there were a number of family pictures around the room, several of which included Beppe. There was a tall girl standing next to him, with honey-colored hair and a distracted scowl. She looked kind of busy.

"Is this your sister?" Ginny asked, pointing at the girl.

"Yes. She is a doctor . . . with babies. I don't know the English for it."

Beppe opened a cabinet under the sink and produced a bottle of wine.

"This is Italy!" he said. "We drink wine here. We'll have some while we wait."

He filled two juice glasses halfway. Ginny sipped at her

wine. It was warm, and she suddenly felt exhausted but also very content. Beppe was talking with his hands now, touching her hand, her shoulder, her hair. Her skin was sticky. She looked out the window at the light blue of the building across the street. The woman from the bed had gotten up and was adjusting her blind and watching them with a detached interest, like she was watching the progress of something cooking in an oven.

"Why do you wear your hair like this?" he asked, holding up a braid and scowling.

"I just always do."

He pulled off the rubber band that held the braid, but Ginny's hair, so well trained (and still a little wet, she guessed), refused to debraid itself.

Her first thought when he kissed her was that it was way too warm for this. She wished there was an air conditioner. And it was so awkward at the kitchen table, leaning across the chairs. But this was kissing. Real, unquestionable kissing. She wasn't sure she wanted to be kissing Beppe, but for some reason, it felt important—like she should be doing it. She was making out with an Italian boy in Rome. Miriam would be proud, and Keith . . . who knew? Maybe he'd be jealous.

Then she realized she appeared to be slipping down out of her chair onto the floor. Not in a falling kind of a way—in a "guided down by Beppe to have more room to make out" kind of way.

This, she really didn't want.

"There is a problem," he said. "What is it?"

"I have to go," she said simply.

151

"Why?"

"Because," she said. "I just have to."

She could see from the baffled look in his eye that he hadn't meant to do anything wrong. He didn't seem to understand.

"Where's your sister?" she asked.

He laughed—not meanly. Like she was a little dim. It annoyed her.

"Come on," he said, sounding conciliatory. "Come sit back down. I am sorry. I should have been more clear. My sister isn't here often."

He started in again. He was giving her quick little kisses on her neck. Ginny craned her head to look out the window, but the woman across the way had lost interest and was gone.

Now Beppe was reaching for the button on her shorts.

"Look," she said, pushing him back, "Beppe . . ."

He was still working at it.

"No," she said, starting to get up. "Stop it."

"Okay. I will leave the button alone."

She pulled herself to her feet.

"Americans," he said dismissively. "All alike."

Her head was thrumming as she raced down the steps. Out on the street, Ginny's sneakers squeaked mercilessly in the humidity. The noise echoed down the narrow street, so much so that diners at a small outdoor café looked up to watch her pass.

Strangely, though the wine had made her groggy, it actually seemed to sharpen her sense of direction. She confidently walked back to the metro station and managed to get herself back to the Colosseum.

The gates were still open, so Ginny went in, weaving her way back through the crumbling things and the half walls, all the way back to the remaining pieces of the virgins.

She grabbed the button that Beppe had been reaching for and yanked it from her shorts. She leaned over the metal bar that kept people back from the statues and tossed it onto the ground between two of the most complete ones.

"Here," she said. "From one virgin to another."

#7
& 8

Dear Ginny,

Head for the train station. You're getting on a night train to Paris.

At least, I'd like you to get on a night train to Paris. They're really nice. But if it's day, get on a day train. Just GET ON A TRAIN.

Why Paris? Paris needs no reason. Paris is its own reason.

Stay on the Left Bank, in Montparnasse. This area is maybe the most famous artists' quarter in the world. Everyone lived, worked, and played here. There were visual artists, like Pablo Picasso, Dégas, Marc Chagall, Man Ray, Marcel Duchamp, and Salvador Dalí. Writers, too, like Hemingway, Fitzgerald, James Joyce, Jean-Paul Sartre, and Gertrude Stein. There were actors, musicians, dancers . . . too many to name. Suffice it to say that if you stood here in the early twentieth century and you started throwing rocks, you would hit a famous and incredibly influential person who helped shape the course of artistic history.

Not that you would have wanted to throw rocks at them.

Anyway, go now.

I have to insist that you go to the Louvre immediately. You can get your next assignment there, in the proper atmosphere.

Love,
Your Runaway Aunt

The Surfboard Sleepers

There were a few seats available on the next train to Paris, much to the surprise of the man who sold Ginny her ticket. He seemed genuinely concerned by her rush and kept asking her why she wanted to leave Rome so soon.

Her little room on the train (the *couchette*) sat six people. The boss seemed to be a middle-aged German woman who had a steel-colored crew cut and a huge supply of oranges. She ate these one after the other, sending visible gasps of orange oil into the air of the cabin as she peeled them, flooding the air with a citrusy smell. At the conclusion of each orange, she'd wipe her hands on the gray fabric of the armrests of her seat. Something about this move gave her a kind of authority.

Under her command were three sleeping backpackers and a man in a lightweight tan suit who had an accent that could have been from absolutely anywhere. To Ginny, he became Mr. Generic Europe. Mr. Generic Europe spent the ride doing a crossword puzzle. He coughed dryly each time the German woman sitting next to him peeled a new orange and then moved his arm so that he didn't get orange pulp on his sleeve when she wiped her hands.

Ginny took out her notebook

July 5
9:56 p.m., train

Dear Miriam,

Last night I had to run from an Italian boy who kept trying to take off my pants. And now I am on a train to Paris. I cannot confirm my identity anymore, Mir. I thought I was Ginny Blackstone, but apparently I have gotten into someone else's life. Someone cool.

About the Italian guy thing, it wasn't particularly sexy or scary. More skanky. He lied to me to get me to go to his sister's apartment, and I went because I am dumb. Then I escaped and had to wander through Rome.

This reminds me of something. I still have a whopping bad case of what you call my scag magnetism. I thought I had gotten rid of it there, but it looks like scary guys still materialize from thin air in my presence. They are drawn to me. I am the North Pole, and they are the explorers of love.

Like the guy with the Radio Shack bag who always hung out outside the second-floor women's bathroom of the Livingston mall who told me on multiple occasions that I look exactly like Angelina Jolie. (Which I do. If you just change my face and body.)

And we can't forget Gabe Watkins, the freshman who dedicated many, many pages of his blog to me and took a picture of me with his phone and Photoshopped his face and mine into a picture of Arwen and Aragorn from Lord of the Rings.

Anyway, you're in New Jersey, and I'm here, speeding through Europe on a train. I realize that maybe this all sounds incredibly exciting, but sometimes it's just really dull. Like now. I have nothing to do on this train (not that writing to you is nothing). I've been by myself for a few days, and it doesn't always feel good.

Okay. I'm going to stop complaining now. You know I miss you, and I promise I'll mail this soon.

Love,

Gin

A few hours into the trip, the woman said something about bed in two languages, and then everyone else in the cabin stood up. There was a lot of pushing around of stuff, and in the process, Ginny got squeezed out of the cabin. When she re-entered, there were six big shelves there. Judging from the fact that Mr. Generic Europe was stretched out on one, Ginny guessed these were supposed to be beds.

There was a lot of awkward shuffling around as people figured out which ones they should take. Ginny got an upper one. Then the German woman snapped out the overhead lights. Some of the others turned on little personal lights that were built into the wall. But Ginny had nothing to read or do, so she remained in the dark, looking at the ceiling.

There was no way she was going to be able to sleep on some jiggling surfboard sticking out of a wall. Especially since the German woman kept sliding open the window, and Mr. Generic Europe kept closing it halfway. Then one of the backpackers said something in Spanish and then said, "Do you mind?" in English and pointed at the window. When she closed it all the way, no one put up a fuss. The German woman opened it again anyway, and the cycle went on throughout the night.

Morning came suddenly, and people started going in and out of the *couchette* with toothbrushes. Ginny rolled over and swung her legs off her surfboard, carefully toeing the ground. When she returned from washing up in the cramped and kind of dark bathroom, the beds were magically folded back into chairs. An hour later, the train stopped and she was shuffling through a huge train station and out onto a wide, sunny boulevard in Paris.

The street signs were little blue plaques on the sides of huge white buildings, frequently obscured by a tree branch, lost in a bunch of other signs, or just impossible to spot. The streets veered off almost constantly. Still, it wasn't that difficult to find a hostel in the neighborhood that Aunt Peg had recommended. It was in a massive building, some kind of old hospital or junior palace. A woman with stiff black curls behind the front desk, after admonishing Ginny for five minutes about not calling ahead in peak season, told her that though there were no singles left, there was plenty of room in the dorms.

"Do you have sheetz?" the woman asked.

"No ..."

"Three euros."

Ginny handed her three euros, and the woman handed her a big white bag made of a rough cotton.

"Eet will be lockout soon," the woman said. "But you may take your sheetz upstairs. You can come back at seex. The door ees locked each night at ten. Eef you are not here at ten, we lock you out. I suggest you take your bag weeth you."

Ginny took her sheet sack up the stairs and went to the room at the end of the hall, as she'd been directed. The door was open just a crack, and she pushed it wide to reveal a very large room with skinny, military-style-looking bunks. The floor was covered in small putty-colored tiles that were still wet from a mopping with a strong-smelling cleanser.

Her roommates were still there, gathering their things for the day. They nodded hello to Ginny and exchanged a few words of greeting, then they went back to their conversation. She quickly concluded that they were from the same high school, which was in Minnesota. She knew this because they all knew one another's names and were talking about what classes they were going to take together. They also kept saying things like, "Oh my God, can you imagine this in Minnesota?" and, "I want to take one of these home to Minnesota."

Ginny put her bag o' sheets on one of the empty cots on the other side of the room. She lingered for a minute, adjusting the sack over the little plastic pad that served as a mattress. She wasn't great with strangers, but today she felt like she could be. If the girls had seemed interested, she could have gotten into a conversation with them. Maybe she could join them, and they could all go somewhere together.

That was it. That was what she wanted. She and the girls

from Minnesota could go through Paris together. They'd go to stores and stop at a café. They'd probably want to go to a club or something. Ginny had never been to a club but knew from her French textbook that that's what you did in Europe. So if the Minnesota girls wanted to go, she would go too. They'd all become good friends really quickly.

But the Minnesota girls had different plans and slipped out the door without her. A screeching voice came over the loud-speaker and told everyone in French and English that they had better get out or there would be some kind of hell to pay. Ginny picked up her bag and left, alone.

Once she was out on the street, she soon passed a metro station with one of the famous, curling green metal entrances and, lacking a better plan, descended. The Paris metro map was a bigger, more troubled cousin of the London map. However, the Louvre was easy to find. The stop was called Louvre. That was a good hint.

Her French textbook had assured her that the Louvre was big, but nothing prepared her for just how big. She waited in line for two hours to get in through the massive glass pyramid entrance. Inside the Louvre, there was a certain safety. It was okay to be a tourist. Everywhere she looked, people were poring over the floor plan, reading guidebooks, digging into backpacks. For once, she fit in completely.

There were three named wings to choose from—Denon, Sully, and Richelieu. She checked her pack into the baggage claim, chose Sully at random, and headed into its depths, immediately finding herself in a re-creation of a stone vault, which led around to the section on ancient Egypt. She wandered through room after room of mummies, tomb decorations, hieroglyphics.

She had always liked Egyptian things, especially as a kid, mostly because she'd seen them at the Metropolitan Museum with Aunt Peg and they played "If you could pick what things you wanted to take with you when you died, what would you take?"

Ginny's list always started off with an inflatable raft. She didn't even own an inflatable raft, but she could imagine it perfectly—it was blue with a yellow stripe and handles. She was convinced that she'd need it in whatever heaven she was imagining.

The Egyptians had also taken some seriously weird crap with them to Deadland. Tables shaped like dogs. Little blue thumb-sized dolls that were supposed to be servants. Big masks of their own heads.

She turned the corner and walked down the hall toward the Roman sculpture.

And she was right back where she started, in the stone vault. It seemed impossible, but it had happened. She tried again, following the signs and the maps. This time, she ended up in the sarcophagus room. On a third try, it looked like she had made it into Roman statues, and then bam, she was right back in with the canopic jars and tomb decorations.

It was like she was walking through some kind of fun house.

She finally had to follow a tour to get out of the land of the dead. She followed them through the Roman statues. Little French children sat below the nudes, gazing up. Not one of them was pointing and laughing. She kept walking through the endless succession of connected chambers until she caught sight of a sign that featured a little picture of the *Mona Lisa* and an arrow. She followed this through at least a dozen more galleries.

One thing Aunt Peg had instilled in her was a comfort around paintings. Ginny never claimed to know much (if anything) about painting. She didn't know a lot about art history, or techniques, or why everyone suddenly fainted in ecstasy if some artist suddenly decided to use only blue. . . . Aunt Peg had explained that while these things were important to some people, the main thing to remember was—they're just pictures. There was no right or wrong way of looking at them, and there was no reason to feel intimidated by them.

As she wandered through the galleries, she felt herself relaxing. There was something about the orderliness of it all—something familiar in this strange place. Just being there made her feel that although she was so far from home, she wasn't alone. It seemed like everyone else was trying to *capture* something about the place. Art students perched everywhere with their massive drawing pads, gazing intently at a work of art or a decoration on the ceiling, trying to duplicate what they were seeing. So many people were taking pictures of the pictures—or weirder still, videotaping them.

Aunt Peg would love that, she thought.

She was so busy watching them that she didn't even realize that she had walked right past the *Mona Lisa*. It had been buried somewhere in one of the crowds. In any case, it seemed as good a time as any to stop. She sat down on a bench in the middle of an Italian gallery with deep red walls and pulled out the next letter.

8

Dear Gin,

So there I was, Gin, on my way from the passions of Rome to the cool romance of Paris.

I thought I was broke before, but I'd always had a little money. But I'd blown most of what I had in Rome.

There was a café I passed almost every day. An amazing smell of fresh bread always came from it, but the place was just falling to pieces--the paint was chipping, the tables were plain and ugly. It was cheap, though. So I went in and had one of the best meals of my life. No one was in there, so the owner sat down and talked to me. He told me that he was closing down the café for a month because everyone in France goes on vacation for a month in the summer. (Another thing that makes France cool.)

I had an idea.

In exchange for a little money for food and letting me sleep in the café, I would redecorate for him. The whole place, top to bottom. For the cost of a couple croque monsieurs, a few hundred cups of coffee, and a little paint, he would have his entire café decorated with original work by a woman who would stay there twenty-four hours a day, seven days a week. It was too good an offer to pass up. So he accepted it.

For the rest of the month, I lived in the café. I managed to get some blankets and pillows and I made myself a little sleeping nest behind the bar. I went to the market for food and cooked my meals in the little kitchen. It didn't really matter if it was day or night--I painted all the time, whenever I felt like it. I slept with the paint fumes. I dreamed about the designs. I permanently stained the skin under my left thumbnail blue. I made curtains from aprons I found in a secondhand shop. I bought up old plates, smashed them in the courtyard out back, and made them into a mosaic.

My Paris was just this tiny room, and a few junk shops, and occasionally walks down the street either at night or when it was raining. This, I thought, is what Paris is all about. Remember, this city is where the peasants seized control and took over and beheaded all of the royals and the rich. It takes pride in the poor artists who have lived here in the past--all the painters, writers, poets, singers who made the bars and cafés famous. Think Les Misérables! Think Moulin Rouge! (But without the TB.) Mari lived on the streets of Paris for three years! She

danced in clubs, and painted on the sidewalk, and
slept wherever she could.

So this is the CHERCHE LE CAFÉ PROJECT. (I know
you take French, but just in case . . . it means
FIND THE CAFÉ.) I want you to find my café based
on what I've told you and what you know about me.

And, of course, when you get there--have
something delicious for me because I am your
loving . . .

STARVING ARTIST AUNT

Ginny looked over at the watch of the man sitting next to her and saw that it was almost six, so she decided to leave. The word *sortie*, which was on signs all over the place, meant "exit." So she followed the signs.

Sortie, sortie, sortie . . .

And then suddenly she was standing in front of the Virgin Megastore, in front of a display for *Star Wars: La Menace Fantôme*.

Did *sortie* mean "This way to Jar Jar"? And why was there a Virgin Megastore in the Louvre?

After ten more minutes of trying unsuccessfully to escape, Ginny finally found the exit. Since the Seine River was right there and there were dozens of bridges over it, she decided to cross. Things were smaller and tighter on the other side. This was the Left Bank, she knew. The student quarter. She glanced around and turned back to walk over the bridge.

Paris seemed to make good on the promise it made in every photograph of it she'd ever seen. People carried long baguettes. Couples walked hand in hand through asparagus-thin streets. And before long, a round moon hung overhead in an electric blue sky and the Eiffel Tower began to twinkle with a thousand little lights. The air was warm, and as Ginny leaned against the side of the Pont Neuf and watched a dinner boat slide along the Seine under her, she thought that this was a perfect Paris night. But she didn't feel perfect. She felt alone, and the only thing she could think of to do was go back to the hostel.

Les Petits Chiens

That night, Ginny sat in the wide, empty lobby, at the long table with the mismatched wooden chairs that held the hostel's computers. Every seat was taken. People from all over hunched intently, reading their e-mails from home, composing epic Web logs, totally unaware of each other's presence.

There was a smell of old smoke from the woman at the front desk's constant sequence of cigarettes. On the wall above Ginny's head were old maps of the world dotted with white star-shaped scars and little holes on the points where they'd been folded time and time again. White stars all over the world, in the oceans. Holes in China, Brazil, Bulgaria. There was even a tiny hole in New Jersey, though much closer to the ocean than where she lived.

For the first time since she'd been away, she had access to the outside. She could write to anyone she wanted—that is, if she didn't follow the rules. The only thing stopping her from talking to Miriam right now was a razor-thin strip of willpower. No electronic communication with America. There was no ambiguity on this point.

But there was nothing in the rules about England. And while she didn't actually have Keith's e-mail address, she guessed it wouldn't be impossible to find. She was good at finding things. She was an Internet bloodhound.

Finding Keith proved to be absurdly easy. She tracked him down through the Goldsmiths site. But it took her a full hour to come up with what she wanted to say to him in her e-mail. It took one hour and about twenty-six versions, in fact, which finally resulted in:

Hey, just wanted to say hi. I'm in Paris right now.

She read it over as soon as she sent it and immediately regretted the "Hey." Why "Hey, just wanted to say hi." Why not just "hi"? Why didn't she tell him she missed him? Why couldn't she say anything cute and clever and alluring? No one would reply to a note like this, because this note was inane.

Except that he did. A reply popped up in her in box. It read simply:

Paris, eh? Whereabouts?

She grabbed her fingers and stroked them to steady them. So, the simple approach had worked. Fine. She would keep it simple:

The UFC Hostel in Montparnasse.

And should she ask him if he was still mad . . . or was she the one who was mad? Maybe better to drop the mad part entirely. Keep it informational.

She waited for half an hour. No reply this time. The night's excitement was over.

She went back upstairs to the dorm, where her roommates were clustered together once again on their side of the room. They smiled at her when she came in, and though she could tell that they had nothing against her, she also sensed that they had been hoping she wasn't coming back. Which was fair enough. They were all friends. They wanted some privacy. She tried to get her things together as quickly and quietly as she could, then climbed into the loudly creaking bunk and tried to sleep.

Ginny bolted straight upright at the loudspeaker announcement at 7:30 a.m., which alerted everyone that breakfast was only until eight thirty and that everyone was expected to be out by nine on the dot.

The Minnesota Contingency was just waking up. They were pulling things out of their bags (much cooler, better-designed bags than her purple-and-green monstrosity). She had nothing, she realized. Nothing except shampoo and toothpaste. That meant no soap and no towel. She had never even thought of it. She dug around in her bag for something she could use as a towel, finally coming up with her fleece.

The bathroom was small, with three shower stalls and four sinks. Though it was fairly clean, there was a raw, rotting smell coming from somewhere deep in the building. She waited in line with the others, slumped against the wall. She noticed that everyone seemed to be staring at her in the mirror. Their eyes flicked back and forth between her towel-fleece and the drawing on her shoulder. For the first time in her life, Ginny felt a little more dangerous than the people around her. It was an interesting feeling, but she figured she would probably have enjoyed it more if it were true.

Also, she had no clean clothes left. Everything was funky and damp and wrinkled. Why she hadn't thought to wash them at Richard's was anyone's guess, but now she had to paw through, looking for the most passable items to put on her still-damp body.

Once she was on the street, Ginny realized that she had no idea how she was supposed to do this. Even just a short walk around the area revealed that Paris was *nothing but cafés*. Cafés everywhere. Cafés and winding streets and broad boulevards. She spent an hour circling the neighborhood, peering into shop windows at displays of bread and pastries, stepping over little dogs, weaving around people intently talking on their phones, and basically accomplishing nothing. Paris was glorious and sunny, of course. But her pack was also heavy, and she had an impossible job to do.

Ginny decided to take a gamble. She walked back to the hostel and tried the heavy black wrought-iron door. It was open. The sound of some heavy piece of cleaning equipment echoed from the hallways somewhere above, bouncing off the marble floors of the lobby. There was a strong smell of fresh smoke.

She cautiously approached the front desk and found the woman still there (Ginny began to wonder if she ever slept), sipping away at a big blue bowl of something and watching *Oprah* dubbed into French. Upon seeing Ginny, she stubbed out her cigarette in anger.

"Eet ees lockout!" she cried. "You are not to be heer."

"I just have a question," Ginny began.

"No. We have rules heer."

"I'm just looking for a café," Ginny said.

"I am not a guidebook!" The *guide* was particularly drawn out and indignant. *Gaaaaaaide.*

"No," Ginny said quickly. "My aunt was a painter. She decorated it."

This calmed the woman a little. She turned back to *Oprah.*

"What ees eet called?" she asked.

"I don't know," Ginny said.

"She did not tell you eets name?"

Ginny decided to sidestep that one.

"This place has a lot of decorations," she said. "And she said it's near here."

"There are a lot oof cafés neer here. I cannot tell you how to find somezing that you do not know ze name of."

"Okay," Ginny said, shuffling to the door. "Thanks."

"Whaight, whaight . . ." The woman waved Ginny over. She took three phone calls and lit a cigarette before explaining why she had called her back.

"Okay. So you go to see Michel Pienette. He sells vegetables at the market. He sells to chefs. He knows all cafés. Explain thees to heem."

She wrote the name down on the back of one of the hostel's cards in big blocky letters: MICHEL PIENETTE.

Though the woman hadn't explained how to get to the market, it was easy enough to find. Ginny could see it in the distance as she got out on the street. Again, this was one of those moments that lived up to her French textbook. There were the heaping tables of fruits and vegetables, the massive breads, the terracotta bowls of fresh olives. It was almost *too* French-textbooky.

After flashing the card around, Ginny managed to find Michel Pienette behind a pyramid of tomatoes. He was smoking a fat cigar and yelling at a customer. There was a short line of people waiting for the same abuse. Ginny took her place behind a man in chef's whites.

"Excuse me," she said to the chef. "Do you speak English?"

"Some."

"Does . . ." She indicated the man with the cigar.

"Michel? No. And he is mean," he said to Ginny. "But his food is good. What do you want?"

"I need to ask him about a café," Ginny said. "But I don't know the name."

"Michel will know. But I will ask for you. Describe it."

"Lots of colors," Ginny said. "It's probably a collage. Maybe made of . . . trash?"

"Trash?"

"Well, kind of . . . trash."

"I will ask him."

The chef waited patiently for his turn, then translated Ginny's question for her. Michael Pienette nodded furiously and chewed on his cigar.

"*Les petits chiens,*" he growled. "*Les petits chiens.*"

That, Ginny knew, meant "the little dogs," which made no sense. The chef seemed to feel this way as well and questioned Mr. Pienette again. This resulted in a minor explosion, and Mr. Pienette spun around and snatched a head of lettuce from another shopper's hand and shouted something over his shoulder.

"He says the café is called The Little Dogs," the chef said. "I think he's getting annoyed. I may not get my eggplant now."

"Does he know where it is?"

He did, but the question made him visibly angrier. He pointed a stubby finger at an alleyway to the left of the market.

"That way," he said. "But please . . . I do need my eggplant."

"Thanks," Ginny said, backing away quickly. "I'm sorry."

The alley was not promising. It was narrow, and the buildings along it were all the same off-white, with small unmarked doorways. Nothing looked like a restaurant. Also, motorcycles kept coming up behind her—actually riding on the sidewalk—to get around the parked cars. So it also seemed like this route might get her killed. Maybe that was what Michel Pienette intended.

But the road widened a bit, and there were a few boutiques and very tiny pastry shops. And then she saw it, a building so tiny that it could hardly have housed four tables. A huge tree sat in front of it, nearly blocking it from view. But it was the window curtains made out of little kitchen aprons that told her this was the place. The front windows were filled with framed clips from magazines, some with pictures. The inside looked to be completely empty, and no lights were on. But when she tried the door, it was open.

It was immediately clear when she got inside why the place was called The Little Dogs. The walls were devoted to the tiny dogs of Paris. Aunt Peg had made a crazy collage of hundreds of magazine pictures of them, then painted around the pictures with big glops of black and hot pink paint. Then, in white, she'd sketched in a few crazy cartoons of poodles. Every table and every chair was painted up in a different set of colors. It seemed like she must have just been working her way through a set of a hundred different tints of paint. Purple with sunny yellow. Lime with candy pink. Fire truck red with navy blue. She spotted the funny Roman orange paired with a deep burgundy.

A man's head popped out from behind the bar, startling Ginny. The French he barked at her sounded vaguely familiar, but it was spoken too quickly and thickly to be understood. She shook her head helplessly.

"We are not serving yet," he said, in English. It was strange how people here knew to do that. It was amazing how they all *could*.

"Oh . . . that's okay."

"Not until dinner. And you need a reservation. Tonight is impossible. Next week, perhaps."

"It's not that," Ginny said. "I'm here to see the decorations."

"You are writing a paper?"

"My aunt did them."

A little bit more of the man was revealed. She could see his shoulders now. "Your aunt?" he asked.

Ginny nodded.

Head, shoulders, most of the chest, and the arms up to the elbows. He was wearing a worn purple T-shirt with a blue-and-white apron thrown loosely over it.

"Your aunt is Margaret?"

"Yes."

Everything changed very quickly. Suddenly, the whole man appeared, and Ginny found herself being forced into a seat.

"I am Paul!" the man said, stepping back behind the bar and producing a small tumbler and a bottle of yellowish liquor. "Wonderful! Let me get you a drink."

After the other night, Ginny had no desire for another drink. "I don't really . . ." she began.

"No, no. Lillet. Very nice. Light. Lovely taste. And a little piece of orange."

He pronounced it *aw-runge*. Plunk. A piece of orange rind went into the glass. He pushed it over and watched intently as Ginny took a cautious sip. It did taste good. Kind of like flowers.

"Now, I will be honest with you," he said, pouring himself some of the Lillet and then sitting opposite her. "I was not so sure about your aunt. She showed me these things that she draws. Little dogs. But wait! Something to eat. Come with me."

He waved Ginny into the kitchen, which was a space the size of a walk-in closet just beyond the bar. And there, as he filled a plate with various items pulled from the refrigerator—cold chicken, lettuces, cheeses—he explained that Aunt Peg's weird paint job had turned a failing four-table restaurant into a highly desirable boutique four-table restaurant with a long reservation list.

"It was a strange thing," he said. "This woman I did not know, offering to stay in my restaurant. To sleep in my restaurant. To make it new, to cover it with pictures of dogs. I should have thrown her out!"

"Why didn't you?" Ginny asked.

"Why?" he repeated. He gazed up and around at the gaily decorated walls. "I do not know why. I suppose she just seemed so sure. She had a way. She had a female charm. . . . You do not take offense at this, you understand. She had a vision, and when she spoke, you believed it. And she was right. Very strange, but right."

Very strange, but right. This was possibly the best description of her aunt that Ginny had ever heard.

After being stuffed with lunch and some apple tart with cream, Ginny was politely booted out so that Paul could get ready for the evening.

"Say hello to your aunt for me!" he said cheerfully. "And come back! Come back often!"

"I will," Ginny said, her smile falling a bit. There was no point in correcting him about Aunt Peg. In his mind, she was still very much alive, and she saw no reason why it shouldn't stay that way for somebody.

She walked back to the hostel in a funk, feeling very annoyed by the late-afternoon crowds and the weight of her bag. For some reason, Paris was not enchanting her right now. It was big and loud and crowded and it had too much stuff in it. The streets were too small. The people talking on their phones too inattentive.

Something about Paul's reaction sank her completely. She wanted to go back to her lonely, creaky bunk, in the room where the other girls ignored her. She wanted to go back there and cry. Just lie there all night and do nothing. There was nothing she could do anyway. She didn't live here. She didn't know anyone.

She pushed open the wrought-iron door roughly and barely noticed when the woman at the desk gave her a slight smile. In fact, she almost didn't recognize the voice that called out to her from the direction of the computers.

"Oi!" it said. "Mad one!"

A Night on the Town

"Where have you been?" Keith greeted her. "I was sitting outside for two hours. Do you know how many dogs tried to . . . never mind."

Ginny was too amazed to speak. It was definitely him. Tall, thin, the reddish brown hair that managed to be both scruffy and perfect, the biking gloves. He smelled just a bit mustier than usual.

"Hello, Keith," he prompted. "How are you? Oh, can't complain."

"Why are you here? I mean . . ."

"One of the tickets you bought for the show," he said. "I took them up to the international office, remember? A French drama student took one. Their school runs a festival and one of their shows fell through, so they asked us to come at the last minute. Packed up the set. Drove over. Fate clearly wants us to be together."

"Oh."

She shifted from foot to foot. Blinked. He was still there.

"I can see you're impressed," he said. "What has your mad aunt got you doing here, anyway?"

"I had to go to a café," she said.

"Café? Now we're talking. I'm starving. We're not performing tonight. We could grab a bite. Unless, of course, you're busy buying out all the seats in the Paris opera house."

Even though she'd just spent the better part of the afternoon eating, Ginny didn't say no. She and Keith spent the next several hours walking. Keith stopped at almost every crepe stand he saw along the way (and there were plenty) and ordered a big, messy pocket filled with everything. He ate as he walked, telling her all about the show. His main news, however, was about David and Fiona, who had gotten back together, much to his disappointment.

It turned dark, and they were still walking. They walked along the river, passing the many bridges. They crossed and walked through a little neighborhood and watched the people at the cafés, who watched them right back. Then they passed by a high fence and what looked like a park.

"Cemetery!" Keith said. "Cemetery!"

Ginny turned to see Keith jumping up, grabbing hold of the top, and shinnying his way over the fence with ease, even with Ginny's pack on his back. He grinned at her from behind the bars.

"Here we go," he said, indicating the dark expanse of monuments and trees on his side.

"Here we go what?"

"It's a Parisian cemetery! They're the best. Five stars."

"What about it?"

"Just come have a look at least."

"We're not supposed to be in there!"

"We're tourists! We don't know better. Come on. Over you go."

"We can't!"

"I've got your bag," he said, turning around to show her. There seemed to be no choice.

"If I come over, promise me we'll just look around and then we'll leave."

"I promise."

It wasn't as easy for Ginny to get over the fence. There was nothing to put her foot against. She had to keep jumping up and trying to grab at the top. At last she got on top of it but had no idea how to get down. Keith finally persuaded her to swing her leg over or she was definitely going to get caught. He almost managed to catch her as she hurled herself down and was very good about helping her off the ground.

"Now," he said, "isn't that better? Come on!"

He ran off into the shadows of the dark trees and statuary. Ginny followed hesitantly and found him perched on a monument shaped like a giant book.

"Have a seat," he said.

She gingerly sat down on the opposite page. Keith tucked his feet up and looked around contentedly.

"Me and my friend Iggy went to this graveyard once . . ." he began, and then stopped.

"About that thing in Scotland, the toy," he said. "Are you still mad about that?"

She wished he hadn't mentioned it.

"Just forget it," she said.

"No. I want to know. I know I shouldn't have taken it. Some old habits die hard."

"That's not a *habit*. Biting your nails is a *habit*. Stealing things is a crime."

"You already gave me this speech. And I already know. I just thought you'd like it."

He shook his head, then pushed himself off the monument.

"Wait," Ginny said. "I know, I just . . . it's stealing. And it was Mari. And Mari was like my aunt's *guru* or something. And I don't steal. I'm not saying you're a bad person, or . . ."

Keith stepped over onto the next grave, which was a flat stone on the ground. He started to jump around and flail his arms.

"What are you doing?" Ginny asked.

"I'm dancing on this guy's grave. You always *hear* about people dancing on your grave, but no one ever does it."

Once he got that out of his system, he came back and stood in front of her.

"You know what you haven't told me?" he asked. "You haven't told me what your aunt died of. I realize this may be a bad place to ask, but . . ."

"A brain tumor," Ginny said quickly, burying her chin in her hands.

"Ah. Sorry."

"It's okay."

"Was she sick for a long time?"

"I don't think so."

"Don't think so?"

"We didn't know," Ginny said. "We only found out afterward."

He sat down next to her again on the other page of the book, then swiveled around to have a better look at it.

"What do you think this is?" he asked. "Hang on."

He leaned in close to the carved letters.

"Come have a look at this," he said. "Turn around."

Ginny turned herself around halfheartedly and looked down.

"What?" she said.

"It's Shakespeare, in French. It's bloody *Romeo and Juliet*. And if I'm not mistaken . . ." He glanced over the writing for a moment. "I think this is part of the crypt scene, where they both die. I'm not sure if this is romantic or creepy."

He picked at the carved letters with his finger.

"Why did you ask me how she died?" Ginny said.

"Don't know," he said, looking up. "It just seemed like a relevant question. And I figured it had to be something . . . well . . . long term. It seems like there was a lot of planning involved with the letters, the money. . . ."

"Did you only want to be around me because of the money?"

He sat up, crossed his legs, and turned to face her directly.

"What exactly does that mean?" he asked. "Is that all you think I was interested in?"

"I don't know. That's why I just asked you."

"The money was nice," he said. "I liked you because you were mad. And you're pretty. And pretty sane for a mad person."

On hearing the word *pretty* (twice, in fact), she drilled her eyes into the carvings. Keith reached over and lifted her chin. He gave her a long look, then slowly slipped his hand behind her neck. Ginny felt her eyes closing, a kind of melting all over her body, and then the sensation of being guided down into the fold of the book next to him. But this time, unlike with Beppe, it wasn't unwelcome or weird. It was just warm.

She wasn't sure how much time had passed when she noticed the light trying to seep in under her closed eyelids. A strong, tightly directed light.

"That can't be good," Keith said again, his mouth still pressed against Ginny's.

A surge of panic ran through Ginny. She sat upright and straightened out her T-shirt. There was a figure of a man standing at the base of the monument. Because he had a flashlight trained on them, it was impossible to see who he was or what he looked like. He spoke to them quickly in French.

"No parlez." Keith scratched at his head.

The man turned the flashlight toward the ground. Once her eyes recovered from the glare, she saw that he was uniformed. He beckoned them down. Keith threw Ginny a grin and slid down, seemingly delighted by the turn of events.

Ginny couldn't move. She tried to dig her fingers into the stone, to clutch onto the shallow letters carved there. Her knees were frozen in a half bend. Maybe the policeman wouldn't see her . . . maybe he was dumb or near blind, and he would think she was part of the sculpture.

"Come on!" Keith said, much too cheerfully for her comfort. He guided her down by the elbow and hoisted up her backpack.

The man walked them down a path, lighting the way with his flashlight. He made no attempts to speak. He led them to a small round guardhouse, where he picked up a walkie-talkie.

"Oh my God," she said, burying her face in Keith's chest to block out the view. "Oh my God. We're getting arrested in France."

"We can only hope," Keith said.

Rapid French. She heard the walkie-talkie land on the desk and pages being flipped in a book. Jangle of keys. Electronic bleeping noise from some kind of sensor. Then they were moving again. She didn't know where, because she decided just to keep her eyes shut and her body tucked in close to Keith's.

There would be phone calls to New Jersey—maybe they would put her on a plane home right now. Or maybe she was going straight to a Parisian jail filled with French hookers with their cigarettes and fishnets and accordions.

Creaking noise. Movement. She clung tighter to Keith, digging her fingers into his arm.

They stopped.

"You can open your eyes now," he said, carefully pulling her fingers back from his arm. "And I'd really like to keep this, if you don't mind."

The Best Hotel in Paris

They were on the sidewalk, and she was still gripping his arm, just not as tightly.

"We're not arrested?" she asked.

"No," he said. "It's *Paris*. You think they arrest people for kissing? Were you worried?"

"A little!"

"Why?"

He seemed genuinely puzzled.

"Because we just got stopped by the French police for public indecency or desecrating graves or something!" she said. "We could have been *deported*."

"Or asked to stop trespassing by the watchman."

They walked along the quiet street of closed-up shops. A neon clock on the outside of a store told them it was just after eleven.

"Oh my God," she said. "I missed curfew. I'm locked out."

"Oh, dear . . ." He pulled a metro ticket from his pocket. "Well, have a good night!"

"You're leaving me?"

"Come on now," he said, jauntily throwing his arm over her shoulders. "Would I do that to you?"

"Probably."

"Come back with me if you want. There's some room on the floor."

The train to where Keith was staying was a suburban commuter train, and that train wasn't running until the morning. He dug his hands into his pockets and smiled.

"So," she said, "what now?"

"We walk around until we find somewhere to sit. And if we like the sitting place, we lie down."

"On the street?"

"Preferably not *on* the street. Preferably on a bench. Maybe some grass. Although, this is Paris. No telling what the millions of little dogs have been doing in the grass. Bench, then. Railway stations are good. I know you said you aren't rich, but now would be a good time to use your secret supply of cash and get us a room at the Ritz."

"My aunt was broke here," she said, almost defensively. "She lived on the floor of a café, behind the bar."

"I was joking," he said. "Relax."

They walked along in silence until they stumbled on one of the more major parks—a real one this time.

"You know where I think we are?" Keith said. "The Tuileries."

Normally, she would have been terrified to come into a park

at night, but after having just been caught by the police in a dark graveyard, the wide avenues and moonlit white fountains didn't seem very alarming. It was hard to see where they were going, but they could follow the crunching noise their footsteps made in a long gravel path they were walking along.

They came to a large circle in the path. There was a fountain in the center and benches all around.

"Here we are," Keith said. "Our hotel. I'll have the bellman take up our bags."

He dropped Ginny's bag down on one of the benches and settled down with his head on one end of it.

"Down pillows," he said. "Sign of quality."

Ginny stretched out in the opposite direction. She stared up at the dark outline of the trees above them. They looked like shadowy hands reaching for the sky.

"Keith?" she asked.

"Yeah?"

"Just checking."

"Still here, mad one."

She grinned.

"Think we're going to get mugged and killed?"

"Hope not."

She wanted to ask something else, but before she could think of what it was, she was asleep.

Ginny heard a rustling by her head, but her body had no desire to move. She had to will her eyes to open. She glanced at her watch. It was ten. Ginny reached over to shake Keith by the shoulder. He had his arms folded and tucked in tight over his chest, and he looked so content that she didn't really want to wake him.

She pulled herself upright and looked around. People were milling around in the park now. No one seemed to pay them any notice. She quickly reached up and rubbed at her face, trying to get rid of any sleep or slobber. She checked her braids as well. They seemed more or less intact. Aside from the fact that she felt a little sticky (which she guessed was something you had to expect after sleeping on a bench all night, though she couldn't really say why), she was in pretty good shape. Total cleanliness had become such a distant reality that her whole perspective on the matter had changed.

Some of the other people in the park were walking dogs or just strolling. No one seemed to care that they'd been using the bench for a bed.

Keith stirred and sat upright slowly.

"Right," he said. "Where's breakfast?"

They found a little café down the street that had a huge pile of pastries in the window. Soon, they were sitting in front of three cups of espresso (all Keith's), a café au lait, and a basket of pain au chocolat.

When he wasn't shoving pastry into his mouth, Keith filled Ginny in on all the news on the show.

"We're just finishing up here," he said, "then we're off to Scotland as soon as we get back. Oh, blimey, that's not the time."

He stood up.

"Look," he said, "sorry . . . but I have to get back. Have a show to do this afternoon. Drop me a line. Let me know how it's going."

He reached over and grabbed her hand, then produced a pen from his pocket.

"Might as well keep it up," he said, writing a few words on the back of her hand. "My IM."

"Okay," she said, unable to hide the dropping in her voice. He grabbed his bag and was out the door. Her body instantly felt heavy. She was alone again. Who even knew if she would ever go back to England and see Keith again?

Automatically, she reached down into the front pouch of the backpack and pulled out the envelopes. The rubber band was growing slack now.

The cartoon on #9 was drawn in dark ink. There was a small drawing of a girl with braids in a skirt in the lower-left corner. Her shadow was long, running on a diagonal across the entire width of the envelope.

She pulled out her notebook.

July 7
10:14 a.m., café table, Paris

Mir,

Keith was HERE. In PARIS. And HE FOUND ME. I know it sounds impossible, but it's true, and it's really not that magical of an explanation. But what matters is that we made out in a graveyard and slept on a park bench.

Just forget it. No way this can be explained on paper. Will require telling in person with lots of gestures. Suffice it to say that I totally love him, and he totally just walked out of the door of the café and I may never see him again . . .

and I know that sounds like a great movie ending, but in life, it just sucks.

I want to follow him. I want to go where his show is and just lie on the sidewalk outside so he can trip over me. Okay? That's how pathetic I am now. You should be thrilled.

I know I have no right to whine. I know that you are still in New Jersey. Please know that I think of you 75 percent of every single day.

Love,
Gin

#9

Dear Ginny,

Know why I like the Netherlands so much?

Because some of it shouldn't even <u>be</u> there.

True story. They constantly keep the sea at bay, and they create new land through drainage and moving dirt around. Water cuts all through the country--and canals slice through Amsterdam. It's a miracle that they keep the place afloat.

You have to be pretty clever to pull that off. Plus, it shows a lot of determination.

It's not surprising that the Dutch also changed painting forever. Back in the 1600s, the Dutch could paint pictures that looked like photographs. They captured light and movement in ways that had never been known before.

These are also people who like to sit around and smoke and drink coffee and dip fries in mayonnaise.

When I finished painting the café, I felt like Paris was done for me. Which is a ridiculous thing to feel, when you think about it. You can't wear out Paris. I guess I'd been in one place for so long (sleeping on the floor behind a bar can be a little confining).

I had a good friend, Charlie, who I knew from

New York. He's an Amsterdam native, and he lives in
a canal house in the Jordaan, which is one of the
coziest, most beautiful quarters in all of Europe. I
decided I needed to see a friendly face, so that's
where I headed. That's where I want you to go.
Charlie will show you the real Amsterdam. His
address is 60 Westerstraat.

There is one other task. You have to go to the
Rijksmuseum, which is the major museum in
Amsterdam. One of the world's great paintings,
Rembrandt's <u>The Night Watch</u>, is there. Find Piet
and ask him about it.

Love,
Your Runaway Aunt

Charlie and the Apple

Amsterdam was damp.

For a start, the central train station was smack in the middle of some kind of inlet and surrounded by water, which seemed to Ginny like somewhere a train station shouldn't be. A canal even separated it from the busy main road that curved past. Ginny made her way over this. From there, countless tiny bridges spanned the canals that spidered out and cut through every street.

Plus, it was raining—a slow, steady drizzle that she could barely see but that soaked her through in minutes.

Paris had been wide, with big, white, wedding-cake-perfect buildings and palaces and things that looked just like palaces even thought they probably weren't. Amsterdam looked like a little village in comparison. Everything was red brick or stone and low to the ground. And the place was swarming—it was a hive. Backpackers, bicyclists, people, streetcars, boats . . . all making their way through the mist.

Westerstraat wasn't far from the train station. (This was according to the free map she had just picked up in the train station. The rules said she couldn't *bring* one but nothing about getting one when she was there. She couldn't believe she hadn't realized this before.) To her amazement, she found the address with little difficulty. (This was what having a map could do.)

The house was one of a row of houses on a canal, with huge front windows and no shades or curtains to hide what was going on inside. Three little pug dogs chased each other around the floor, and she could see massive abstract oil paintings hanging on the walls, a room full of overstuffed furniture and thick rugs, and cups of coffee on a low table. Hopefully this meant Charlie was home, because if Charlie was home, she would soon be warm and dry.

As she knocked on the door, she could almost feel the change of clothes. Socks first, then maybe pants. Her shirt was still somewhat dry under her fleece.

A young Japanese man answered the door when she knocked and said something in Dutch.

"Sorry," she said slowly. "English?"

"I'm American," he answered, smiling. "What can I do for you?"

"Are you Charlie?"

"No. I'm Thomas."

"I'm looking for Charlie," she said. "Is he home?"

"Home?"

Ginny checked the address on the letter again, then looked at the number above the door. They matched. But just to be certain, she held the paper over to Thomas.

"Is this here?" she asked.

"That's the right address, but nobody named Charlie lives here."

Ginny wasn't quite sure how to process this information. She stood dumbly in the doorway.

"We just moved in last month," he said. "Maybe Charlie was here before?"

"Right." Ginny nodded. "Well, thanks."

"Sorry."

"Oh, no." She did a quick check of her face to make sure she didn't look like she was going to burst into tears. "It's not a problem." Few things Ginny had ever experienced seemed gloomier than slogging back alone from Westerstraat with no particular destination in mind, in what was rapidly becoming actual rainfall. The gray sky seemed to hang about two feet over the tops of the low buildings, and every time she swerved to avoid one bike, another seemed to take aim for her. Her pack grew heavier from the soaking, and little rivulets were running down her face and over her eyes. Soon she was so wet that it ceased to matter. She would never be dry again. This was permanent.

The point of being here in Amsterdam appeared to have just slipped away, aside from a short trip to a museum. Whatever wisdom that Charlie was supposed to impart was gone.

There was no shortage of hostels in the area around the station. They were all a little sketchy looking, with signs that looked more like they were for skateboard shops than places to stay. She tried a few, but they were all full. Finally, she went into one called The Apple.

The front of The Apple was a small café. There were several old sofas, along with lawn decorations—plaster cupids, birdbaths filled with hard candy, pink flamingos. There was a reggae album playing, and the sweet tang of cheap incense hung in the air. A bright stripe of green, yellow, and orange—the colors of the Jamaican flag—ran along the wall, along with several posters of Bob Marley hung at odd angles.

It was like living in a stoner's locker.

This café also served as a front desk. They did have room, as long as Ginny was willing to pay for two nights up front.

"Room fourteen," the guy said, scrawling something on an index card. "Third floor."

Ginny had never seen a set of stairs this steep in her life—and there were about a million of them. She was completely out of breath by the time she reached her floor, which was only three stories up. The room numbers were each inside pictures of pot leaves painted on the doors. It was only when she was standing in front of room fourteen that she realized that she hadn't been given a key. She soon knew why—the door had no lock.

What hit Ginny first was the powerful smell of mildew and the uneasy knowledge that if she touched the carpet, it would probably feel damp. There were way too many beds in the room, each covered with a plastic overlay. A girl was standing at one of these, hastily shoving stuff into her bag. She pulled it onto her back and made her way quickly to the door.

"Make sure they give you your deposit back," she said on her way out. "They'll try to keep it."

A quick look explained a lot. Previous tenants had left their comments for all to read. There were scrawls all around the walls, little messages of doom like, MY PASSPORT WAS STOLEN FROM RIGHT HERE (with a little arrow), *Welcome to Motel Hell, Thanks for the lepprosey!* and the philosophical, *Stay stoned and you may be okay.*

Everything was broken—either slightly or completely. The window didn't open very far, nor would it close. There was no lightbulb in the one overhead light. The beds were like wobbly restaurant tables, balanced out with bits of cardboard. Some had strange objects in place of an entire leg, and one of the bunks was just completely collapsed. Above this bed someone had written in huge letters: HONEYMOON SUITE.

She ran in and out of the bathroom before her brain could take a good snapshot of the horrors she found within.

The best bed on offer seemed to be the one that the stolen passport arrow was pointing at. It had all four of its own legs, and the mattress seemed relatively clean. At least she couldn't see any marks through the plastic (which wasn't the case with some of the others). She quickly threw the sheet over it so she wouldn't be able to look at it too closely.

The locker at the end of her bed had no lock, and one of the hinges was busted. She opened it up.

There was a *thing* in it.

The thing might have been a sandwich at some point, or an animal, or a human hand . . . but what it was now was fuzzy and putrid.

A minute later, Ginny was down the stairs, out the door, and gone.

Homeless, Homesick, and Diseased

There was nothing left to do but eat.

She squelched into a little grocery store and looked over the rows and rows of chips and gummy bears. She grabbed a huge bag of some kind of waffle cookie called a Stroopwaffle that was on sale. They looked like tiny waffles stuck together with syrup. It was kind of like comfort food. She took her cookies outside and sat on a bench and watched the low flat boats and the bicyclists go by. There were disgusting smells that she couldn't get out of her nose. An uneasy sensation crept all over her skin—a feeling of permanent contamination.

Nothing seemed clean. The world would never be clean again. She shoved the bag into her pack unopened and went searching for another place to stay.

Amsterdam was full. Ginny walked into every place she

could find that seemed at least a little safer than The Apple. The only places that had any room at all were way out of her price range. By seven o'clock, she was getting desperate. She had walked pretty far from the city center.

There was a small canal house made of sandy-colored stone with white curtains and flowers in the windows. It looked like the kind of house a cute little old lady might live in. She would have passed it by, if not for the blue electric sign that said: HET KLEINE HUIS HOSTEL AND HOTEL AMSTERDAM.

This was her last try. If this failed, she could go back to the train station knowing she had done all she could. Not that she knew where she would go from there.

Because of her backpack, she had to squeeze sideways into the narrow hall, which led to a lobby that wasn't much more than a hallway itself. There was a cutaway window, behind which was a desk, and behind that was a neat family kitchen. A man came out to help her and apologized, but he had nothing left. He had just rented the very last room.

"Don't you have anywhere to stay?" It was an American voice. She turned to see a man on the stairs, a guidebook in his hand.

"Everything's pretty full," she said.

"Are you on your own?"

She nodded.

"Well, we can't let you back out in the rain with no place to go. Hold on."

He went back up the stairs. Ginny wasn't sure what she was holding on for, but she waited anyway. He came back again a moment later, a wide grin on his face.

"Okay," he said, "it's settled. Phil can stay in our room with us, and you can share the other room with Olivia. We're the Knapps, by the way. We're from Indiana. What's your name?"

"Ginny Blackstone," she said.

"Well, hi, Ginny." He extended his hand, and Ginny shook it. "Come meet the family! You're with us now!"

Olivia Knapp, Ginny's new roommate ("Her initials are OK!" Mr. Knapp had said. "So just call her OK, okay?"), was a tall girl with short golden blond hair. She had wide, doe-like blue eyes and a creepily even, toast brown tan. The whole family was kind of like that—short hair, whippet thin, dressed exactly as the guidebooks recommended, in easy-to-maintain, modest, all-weather clothes.

The room she was to share with Olivia was a far cry from the one she had hastily vacated that morning. It was an extremely narrow room, but it was clean and decorated in a soft, girlish style, with rose-and-cream-striped wallpaper and a pitcher filled with pink and red tulips sitting on the windowsill. Best of all, it had two beds made up in fluffy white comforters that still held the lingering scent of detergent.

Olivia wasn't much of a talker. She had tossed her things down on the bed and rapidly unpacked. (It was a textbook packing job, Ginny noticed. Every inch of the bag perfectly utilized. No overpacking.) She filled two of the four dresser drawers and then nodded to Ginny, indicating that the other two were hers. If she thought it was weird that her parents had just taken on a complete stranger for five days, she didn't show it. In fact, Ginny quickly got the impression that this kind of thing happened to them a lot, and they simply didn't notice it anymore. Olivia flopped on the bed, put her earphones in, and stretched her legs up to the ceiling. She didn't stir until Mrs. Knapp came and got them for dinner.

Even though she hadn't eaten all day, food still didn't seem like a good idea to Ginny. The Knapps tried to persuade her for a few minutes but eventually bought the "I've been traveling for a while and haven't had any sleep" excuse.

When they were gone, she wasn't even quite sure why she hadn't gone with them. Something in her just wanted to stay in this little room. She opened her pack and pulled out her wet clothes (waterproofing only did so much). She arranged these over the nightstand.

She went into the bathroom and took a long, scalding hot shower. (Soap! Towels!) She made a careful effort not to scrub at her ink tattoo, which was starting to fade just a little.

She sat down on her bed, enjoying the warm flush on her skin and the feeling of clean, and wondered what to do next. She looked around the room. She could try to wash some clothes in the sink. (She hadn't washed anything since London, and it was becoming a problem.) She could go out. But then she saw them—Olivia had books and magazines and music just *sitting there on her bed.*

From the way Olivia had carefully set out her things, Ginny was more than a little leery of touching anything. And it wasn't in Ginny's nature to use something that didn't belong to her without asking.

But what could it hurt to look at a book or listen to music a few minutes, especially since she really hadn't had anything to listen to or read in about three weeks?

The temptation was too great.

She locked the door and carefully studied the exact arrangement of all the items. She tried to code it all in her mind. The magazines were lined up with the third pink stripe from the bottom of the bed. The earphones were resting in a stethoscope shape, with the right one just a little below the left.

Olivia's music choices were more edgy than Olivia herself appeared to be. Ginny listened to it all, the folky stuff and electronica . . . She paged through the glossies hungrily. It was all so new, so fresh. She didn't even read these kinds of magazines at home, but now, she was totally content examining the lipstick ads and reading about the best bangs for her bikini buck.

There was a rattling at the door. A knocking. Ginny ripped the earphones out in a panic and fell off the bed in her haste to rearrange them on Olivia's side as she had found them. Right earbud above left? No. Whatever . . . She threw them down and smacked the magazines next to them. She had just enough time to pull her hands away from Olivia's stuff before the door swung open.

"What are you doing on the floor?" Olivia asked.

"Oh, I . . . fell out of bed," Ginny said. "I was asleep. I got startled. Did you come back early . . . or what time is it?"

"My parents started talking to some people," Olivia said, unenthused. She glanced at the things on her bed. She didn't register any suspicion, but she kept her gaze there for a while. Ginny pulled herself up by the blanket and climbed back into her bed.

"So, OK . . ."

"Nobody calls me that," Olivia said sharply.

"Oh."

"Your clothes are all over the place."

"They got wet," Ginny said, feeling an odd wave of guilt for being so damp. "I'm trying to dry them."

Olivia didn't reply. She picked up her iPod, turning it over and examining it closely. Then she stuck it in the front pocket of her bag and loudly pulled the zipper. It sounded like the angry growl of a massive bee. Then she vanished into the bathroom. Ginny rolled toward the wall and squeezed her eyes shut.

Life with the Knapps

"Rise and shine, porcupines!"

It took a tremendous effort for Ginny to unglue her eyelids. She had been sleeping so peacefully, and the light was soft coming in through the little curtains. And though her bed was narrow, it was so clean and cozy.

Now a hand was on her leg, shaking her.

"Up and Adam, Miss Virginia!"

Across from her, Olivia was swinging out of bed with robotic discipline. Ginny looked up and saw Mrs. Knapp standing over her, wielding a plastic travel mug. She put a paper on the pillow next to Ginny's head.

"Today's schedule," she said. "Lots to do! So let's get bright eyed and bushy tailed!"

She yanked the curtains open and switched on the overhead light. Ginny winced and blearily looked at the paper. The top of the page read: DAY ONE: MUSEUM DAY I. There was a chart of activities and times, beginning at 6:00 a.m. (wake up) and running down to 10:00 (off to bed!). In between were at least ten separate events.

"Meet you guys downstairs in half an hour?" Mrs. Knapp chirped.

"Yeah," Olivia said, already halfway into their little bathroom.

An hour later, they were waiting in the plaza in front of the Rijksmuseum—apparently, the biggest, baddest museum in Amsterdam—just before it opened. Ginny tried to take in the grandness of the building and ignore the fact that a number from *42nd Street* was being discussed and there was a very real chance that the Knapps were going to start dancing. Fortunately, the museum opened before this nightmare could become a reality.

The Knapps had a very clear idea of how they planned to tackle the Netherlands' most comprehensive collection of art and history—they were going to make a series of well-planned strikes. This was an *operation*.

As soon as they got inside, they asked the person at the information desk to circle the really important things that they had to see. Then they tore off, guide in hand. They speed walked through a display of four hundred years of Dutch history, pointed at some blue-and-white Dutch pottery. Once they got to the art wing, it became a game of speed tag. The mission was simply to find the paintings on their guide, stare at them, then run as quickly as they could to the next one.

Luckily, the third stop was Rembrandt's *The Night Watch*. There was no problem finding it because signs everywhere pointed to it (and unlike in the Louvre, the signs seemed to be telling the truth). Plus, the painting was massive. It took up a good chunk of a wall, stretching almost to the ceiling. Amazing, the people in the painting looked life-sized, though it wasn't really clear to Ginny what they were doing. It seemed to be a gathering of noblemen with big hats and ruffles around their necks, plus some soldiers with huge flags, and a few musicians for good measure. Most of the painting was dark, the figures in shadow. But a sharp wedge of light cut through the middle, illuminating a figure in the center, dividing the canvas into three triangular sections.

("When in doubt," Aunt Peg had always said, "look for the triangles in the paintings." Ginny had no idea why this was important, but sure enough. Triangles everywhere.)

"Pretty neat," Mr. Knapp said. "Okay. Next is something called *Dead Peacocks*. . . ."

"Can I stay here, then meet you?" Ginny asked.

"But there are so many paintings to see," Mrs. Knapp said.

"I know, but . . . I'd really like to look at this one."

The Knapps weren't getting this *at all*. Mr. Knapp looked down at his guide with its many circles.

"Okay . . ." he said. "Meet you at the entrance in an hour."

One hour. That seemed like enough time to find Piet. What was a Piet? Piet was probably a person, since she had to ask the Piet something. Okay. *Who* was a Piet?

She examined all of the title plates of the paintings first. No Piets. She sat on the bench in the middle of the room and looked around at the crowd shuffling past *The Night Watch*. Obviously, no one knew when she would be here, so Piet wasn't coming here specifically to meet her. She walked through all of the adjoining exhibition rooms, read all of the title plates. She poked her head around corners, checked in the bathrooms. No Piets anywhere.

She had no choice but to give up and rejoin the Knapps, who had absorbed the massive museum to their satisfaction. They headed to the Van Gogh Museum. Mrs. Knapp had scheduled only an hour for this, but even this was too much for them. They looked weary in the face of such swirling, hallucinogenic paintings. Mr. Knapp also felt these were "something" and mumbled, "What was *he* on?"

They had to take a tram to get to their next museum, the Rembrandt House Museum, which was (as the name suggested) Rembrandt's house, and kind of dark and creaky. The Maritime Museum came next (2:30–3:30; boats, anchors). They had from four until five to see the Anne Frank house. This got a serious "something" from Mr. Knapp, but it didn't slow down their furious pace, since they had to get back to the hotel for "Knapptime" (5:30–6:30). Once they got back, Olivia dropped onto her bed, rubbed at her legs furiously, stuck her earphones in her ears, and fell asleep. Ginny stretched out as well, and even though she was exhausted, she couldn't rest. Just as she felt herself drifting off, the door flew open, and they were on their way again.

They had dinner at the Hard Rock Café, almost all of which was occupied with a discussion of Phil's fabulous girlfriend. They'd never been separated before, so Phil had to take a break at the end of dinner to call her. When he was gone, Mr. and Mrs. Knapp switched topics to talk about Olivia's running. Running was Olivia's *thing*. She ran in high school, and she had just finished her freshman year of college. She was a nursing major, but mainly, she ran. While they were away, Olivia was looking forward to doing some running. Olivia didn't say any of this herself. She just ate her grilled chicken salad and scanned the room in steady right-to-left movements.

After that, they had to hurry to catch a glass-topped sightseeing boat for a night cruise, during which the Knapps did a few highlights from *Phantom of the Opera*. (Specifically, they explained, the boat scene.) They weren't as loud as they had been in the morning; they were sort of singing to themselves. And then, mercifully, the day ended.

Contact of Various Kinds

For the next three days, Ginny followed the Knapps' grueling schedule. Every morning, at the crack of dawn, there was a knock, a shake, some unwelcome cheer, and a printed page on her pillow. Every bit of Amsterdam was broken into carefully scheduled increments. The museums. The palace. The Heineken factory. Every quarter. Every park. Every canal. Every night, she listened to Mr. Knapp say something like, "You know, even if you had a whole month, you still couldn't do this city justice."

Ginny almost wept with joy when she found out that day five on the Knapp Tour of Amsterdam had been marked down as a "free day." Phil vanished after breakfast, and by eight, Olivia was already changing into her special high-tech running clothes. Ginny sat on the bed and watched, trying to convince herself not to lie back down and go to sleep for the entire day. She still had to find the mysterious Piet and also to send a note to Keith. She'd been wanting to for days but hadn't managed to escape long enough to do it.

"What are you doing today?" Olivia said.

Ginny looked up with a start.

"I was . . . going to send some e-mail," she said.

"So was I, after my run. There's a big Internet café a few streets over. I'm going there later. If you want, we can split a day pass. It's cheaper that way."

Olivia provided directions to the Internet café, and Ginny went over—after allowing herself a long shower and a chance to carefully braid her hair.

After sending Keith a note, Ginny switched on the messenger program and then killed an hour or so just surfing. It felt like . . . drugs . . . even better than the magazine and music a few nights before. It almost scared her how much she missed looking at the same stupid sites.

There was a bleep as Keith came online.

well how is a'dam?

Adam? she wrote.

amsterdam you twit.

Suddenly, Miriam's IM profile lit up as well.

OH MY GOD ARE YOU THERE? she wrote.

Ginny almost screamed. She immediately put her fingers on the keys to answer, then drew them back, as if she had been scalded.

She couldn't communicate with anyone from the U.S. online.

WHY AREN'T YOU ANSWERING? Miriam wrote.

YOU CAN'T WRITE TO ME, CAN YOU?

OH MY GOD.

OKAY.

IF YOU'RE THERE, LOG ON AND LOG OFF REALLY FAST.

She tried to quickly log on and off, but the computer was slow. She groaned in frustration. When she finally came back, a few messages from Keith quickly popped up.

hello?

do I offend?

where did you go?

have to go anyway

No, I am here . . . she wrote.

But it was too late. He was already off.

Miriam was still there, though, cyber-screaming.

I AM TOUCHING THE SCREEN. I MISS YOU SO MUCH.

Ginny felt her eyes tearing up. This was so stupid. Her best friend was right there, and Keith was gone.

She put her fingers on the keys. She started typing quickly, one line after another.

I'm not supposed to do this but I can't stand it

I miss you too

things are so complicated

ARE YOU OKAY?

Fine.

I GOT YOUR LETTERS. WHERE IS KEITH? DO YOU LOVE HIM?

I think he's still in Paris. He's just Keith.

WHAT THE HELL DOES THAT MEAN? I SO WANT TO COME THERE.

It means I'll probably never see him again.

219

WHY NOT?

Ginny jumped to see Olivia suddenly sitting next to her.

"Done?" she asked.

"Um . . ."

Olivia looked kind of impatient, and Ginny's guilt reflex managed to kick in.

I have to go. I miss you.

MISS YOU TOO.

A few minutes later, after giving the computer to Olivia, she was back out on the street. The sudden contact left her numb, and she had a hard time uprooting herself from her spot on the sidewalk, so bikes and backpackers and people on cell phones wove around her.

There was still something to be done. Where was Piet? Who was Piet? Piet was somewhere back at the museum, so that's where Ginny headed . . . back to the massive Rijksmuseum.

What had she missed? What else was there? Paintings. People. Names.

And guards.

Guards. The people who looked at the paintings all the time. The guard in this room was a sage-looking old man with a white beard. Ginny went up to him.

"Excuse me," she said. "Do you speak English?"

"Of course."

"Are you Piet?"

"Piet?" he repeated. "He's in seventeenth-century still life. Three rooms down."

Ginny practically ran down the hall. There was a young guard with a tiny goatee standing in the corner of the room, playing with his belt buckle. When asked if he was Piet, he narrowed his eyes and nodded.

"Can I ask you about *The Night Watch*?"

"What about it?" he asked.

"Just . . . about it? Do you guard it?"

"Sometimes," he said, eyeing her suspiciously.

"Did a woman ever ask you about it?"

"Lots of people ask me about it," he said. "What do you want?"

Ginny didn't know what she wanted.

"Just anything," she said. "What you think about it."

"It's just part of my life," he said with a shrug. "I see it every day. I don't think about it."

That couldn't be it. This was Piet. This was *The Night Watch*. But Piet just scratched at his lower lip and scanned the room, already detached from the conversation.

"Right," she said. "Thanks."

Back at Het Kleine Huis, Ginny dug through her bag and tried to figure out which of her clothes were the cleanest—which was a tough call.

"I've got some great news!" Mrs. Knapp said, bursting through the door without knocking, startling Ginny. "Something big for our last day together! A bike ride! To Delft! Our treat!"

"Delft?" Ginny asked.

"It's one of the other big towns. So, lots of rest tonight! We'll be getting up early! Tell Olivia the good news!"

Bang. Door shut. She was gone.

The Secret Life of Olivia Knapp

Early the next morning, they were on a tram out to the far edge of Amsterdam. Ginny liked the tram. It was like an overgrown toy train that had gotten loose on the streets. She looked out the window and saw the Netherlands wobbling by—its ancient houses and constant canals and people in practical shoes.

One thing that the Knapps hadn't said but Ginny could abundantly feel (really feel—like it was physically coming in through the back of her head) was that though they liked her enough, they were glad that she wasn't their child. Or rather, if she had been, things would have been different. She would have been roboting herself out of bed at six in the morning *automatically*. She wouldn't have dragged her feet on the mad rush from place to place. She would have sung show tunes. She would have liked running or at least *thinking* about running. And she definitely would have been more excited about riding a bike for fifteen miles. She knew this last one for certain because they kept asking her, "Aren't you excited, Ginny? A bike ride? Isn't that great? Aren't you excited?"

Ginny said that she was excited, but she also kept yawning, and the expression on her face probably told the whole story: she didn't like bikes. In fact, she hated bikes. She hadn't always hated bikes. She and Miriam had gone everywhere on their bikes when they were kids, but that had all stopped one day when they were twelve, and Ginny's bike decided not to stop as she took a big hill and she was forced to turn hard and wipe out on the asphalt to keep from running into traffic.

She tried not to think about this as she was being saddled onto a bike that was much too big for her. The tour director said it was because she was such a "big—I mean tall big— girl." So that meant all the shorter people got bikes that were right for their height, and she got the big girl bike that was left.

And she wasn't even that tall, anyway. Olivia was taller.

This was obviously "single Ginny out" day.

The ride to Delft was fairly easy, even for her, since the Netherlands was flat as a board. She only felt herself teetering off her towering bicycle once or twice, and that was only when she sped up a little to put some distance between herself and the Knapps, who were singing every song they could think of that referenced bikes, or riding, or going somewhere.

Delft turned out to be a beautiful town, a miniature version of Amsterdam. It was one of those places so absurdly cool that Ginny knew that either through legalities or luck, she would never, ever be able to live there. The citizenry simply would not permit it.

Also, they had wooden shoes in one of the first shops they got to. Mrs. Knapp was thrilled. Ginny just wanted to sit down, so she crossed the street (the canal, really) and sat down on a bench. To her surprise, Olivia joined her.

"Who were you writing to yesterday?" Olivia asked.

Maybe it was the shock of Olivia showing a sudden burst of actual personality that caused what happened next.

"My boyfriend," Ginny said. "I was writing to my boyfriend, Keith."

Okay. So she was lying, kind of. She didn't even know *why* she was lying. Maybe just to hear it out loud. Keith . . . *my boyfriend.*

"I thought so," Olivia said. "I was doing that too. I can't call like Phil."

"Why can't you call your boyfriend?"

"No." Olivia shook her head. "It's not like that."

"Not like what?"

"It's just . . . I have a girlfriend."

From across the street, Mr. and Mrs. Knapp were gesturing wildly, pointing down to their feet. They were each wearing brightly colored wooden shoes.

"My parents would off themselves if they knew," Olivia said meditatively. "They'd totally hang themselves from the rafters. They notice everything but what's right in front of them."

"Oh . . ."

"Does that freak you out?" Olivia said.

"No," Ginny said quickly. "I think it's great. You know. That you're gay. It's great."

"It's not a big deal."

"No," Ginny corrected herself. "Right."

Mr. Knapp broke into a little dance. Olivia sighed. They sat in silence for a few minutes, watching the embarrassing spectacle. Then the Knapps disappeared into another store.

"I think Phil's guessed," Olivia said glumly. "He keeps asking me about Michelle. Phil's kind of an asshole . . . I guess. I mean, he's my brother. But still. Don't say anything."

"I won't."

After her sudden confession, Olivia lapsed right back into being Olivia, with her middle-distance stare and the constant rubbing of her legs.

"I think they're buying cheese," she said after a moment, and got up and went across the bridge.

Ginny sat perfectly still for a moment and watched the boats rocking in the canal. The amazing part wasn't exactly that Olivia was gay—it was that Olivia had *feelings* and *things to say* and that she'd said them. There was something under that emotionless gaze of hers.

Olivia had just hit on something as well . . . not the thing about the cheese, but about not noticing what's right in front of you. Like Piet—he saw *The Night Watch* every day and never really looked at it. What was in front of her? Boats. Some water. Some old canal buildings. Her oversized bicycle that she was going to have to ride all the way back to Amsterdam, probably getting herself killed in the process.

What was she doing? There was no hidden message here. Aunt Peg had screwed this one up. There was no Charlie. Piet was clueless. And now she was reduced to trying to string together some kind of theory about what this was all about—a theory based on nothing but snippets of conversation.

Amsterdam, she had to admit to herself, was just a washout.

For their final night in town, the Knapps had decided to go to a restaurant that was in a medieval bank that looked like a tiny castle. There were torches on the stone walls and suits of armor in the corners. Olivia seemed tapped out from her confession earlier in the day and stared at one of these for the entire meal, never once speaking.

"So," Mrs. Knapp said, producing a sheet of paper, which she set on the table. "I've written up a little list for you, Ginny. We'll say twenty euros for tonight's dinner, just to make things easy."

She wrote something on the bottom and then passed the paper to Ginny. All along, the Knapps had been dropping their credit card for everything. Ginny had been aware that she was going to have to contribute at some point. That point had obviously come in the form of this very carefully itemized list of every ticket and every meal, plus the cost of her part of the hotel.

Ginny certainly didn't mind paying for herself, but there was something odd about having the bill passed to her in the middle of dinner, with all four Knapps looking on. She felt too self-conscious to even look at it. She put in on her lap and pulled the edge of the tablecloth over it.

"Thanks," she said. "I'll need to go to the ATM, though."

"Take your time!" Mr. Knapp said. "In the morning."

So why, Ginny wondered, *did you give it to me now?*

Back at the Huis, Ginny read over the list and realized that she hadn't been paying any attention at all to how much this was costing. They didn't ask for the full amount for the room (it turned out that they had the nicest rooms in the place, which cost a lot more), but it still came to two hundred euros for the five days. Along with the frightening pace of their sightseeing (all of those admissions added up), the restaurants, the Internet café—she had burned through almost five hundred euros. She was fairly sure that she had five hundred euros left, but the sliver of doubt gave her a sleepless night. She was up before anyone, and she slipped out to make sure.

The ATM gave her the money, which was a relief, but it wouldn't tell her what her balance was. It just spat a handful of purple notes at her, then winked off with a message in Dutch. It could have said, "Screw you, tourist!" for all she knew.

She sat down on the sidewalk and pulled out the next envelope. Inside, there was a postcard, painted in swirling watercolors. It seemed to be a view of the sky, but there were two suns—one containing a 1 and the other a 0.

Letter ten.

"All right," she said, "what now?"

#10

Dear Ginny,

Let's not be precious about it, Gin. We haven't talked about it so far, and it's about time we did. I got sick. I am sick. I will continue to get sicker. I don't like it, but that's the truth--and it's always better to face things head-on. Rich words coming from me, but accurate ones.

When I stopped before going into the Empire State that November morning--there was a reason. It wasn't just because I felt moral indignation at the thought of working in the building. I had forgotten the suite number of the office where I was going. I'd left it at home.

The other version made for a better story . . . that I stopped dead, turned around, left. That's romantic. It's not quite the same if I said I just had a brain fart, left my Post-it, and had to turn around.

Looking back, Gin, I think that was the beginning. It was little things like that. I've always been a little flaky, I admit, but there was a definite pattern going on. Little facts were just getting winked away now and then. My doctors tell me that this problem I have is fairly recent, that there's no way I would have seen symptoms two years ago, but doctors aren't always right. I think I knew that time was soon going to become an issue.

When I was in Amsterdam with Charlie, I definitely knew something was wrong with me. I wasn't sure what. I thought it was something with my eyes. It was the quality of the light. Sometimes things seemed very dark. There were little black spots in my vision, spots that would sometimes eat up my view. But I was too chicken to go to the doctor. I said it was nothing and decided instead to keep moving. My next stop was an artists' colony in Denmark.

So, your next instruction is to take a plane to Copenhagen, immediately. It's a short trip. Send an e-mail to knud@aagor.net with flight information. Someone will meet you at the airport.

Love,
YRA

The Viking Ship

She was standing in the airport in Copenhagen, staring at a doorway, trying to figure out if it was (a) a bathroom and (b) what kind of bathroom it was. The door merely said *H*.

Was she an *H*?

Was *H* "hers"? It could just as easily be "his." Or "Helicopter Room: Not a Bathroom at All."

She turned around in despair, her pack almost causing her to lose her balance and tumble over.

The Copenhagen airport was sleek and well organized, with shiny metal plates on the walls, metal strips along the floors, and big metal columns. All airports were kind of sterile places, but the Copenhagen airport was like an operating table. Looking through the massive glass panels that lined the building, Ginny could see that the sky outside was also a steely gray.

She was waiting for someone she didn't know and who didn't know her. She only knew that he or she wrote English in all caps and told her to WAIT BY THE MERMAIDS. After a lot of walking around in semicircles (the whole place was one big curve) and asking a lot of people, she found statues of two mermaids looking over from one of the second-floor rails. She had been standing next to them for over forty-five minutes, she badly needed to pee, and she was seriously wondering whether this was some kind of test.

Just as she was about to make a run for the *H* room, she noticed a tall man with long brown hair approaching her. She could see that he wasn't very old, but his big brown beard gave him a mature, imposing air. His outfit—a pair of jeans, a Nirvana T-shirt, and a leather jacket—was normal, except for the belt of chain-link metal that hung from his waist, with various objects hanging off it like charms, like a large animal tooth and something that looked like a massive whistle. And he was making a beeline for her. She looked around, but she had a pretty strong feeling that he wasn't charging toward the group of Japanese tourists who were converging next to her under a small blue flag.

"You!" he called out. "Virginia! Right!"

"Right," Ginny said.

"I knew it! I am Knud! Welcome to Denmark!"

"You speak English?"

"Of course I speak English! All Danes speak English! Of course we do! And pretty good English!"

"Pretty good," Ginny agreed. There was an exclamation point after everything Knud said. He spoke English *loudly*.

"Yes! I know! Come on!"

Knud had a very modern, very expensive-looking blue BMW

motorcycle with a sidecar waiting for them in the parking lot. The sidecar, he explained, was what he used to transport all of his tools and materials (what they were, he didn't say). He was absolutely certain her massive backpack would fit in there as well, and he was right. A moment later, she was in the sidecar, low to the ground, tearing down the street of yet another European city that looked (she was ashamed to admit it—it seemed like such a cop-out) very much like the one she had just left.

He parked his bike on a street full of colorful houses, all linked together, that sat along a wide canal. Ginny had to wait until she was unpacked and then stepped uncertainly out of the sidecar. She took a step in the direction of the buildings, but Knud called her back.

"This way, Virginia! Down here!"

He was carrying her pack down a set of concrete steps that led down to the water. He continued down the sidewalk that was along the very edge of the canal, past several carefully marked out "parking spots" where large houseboats were docked. He stopped at one of these. His was a complete little house that looked like a small wooden cabin. There were flower boxes full of red flowers at the windows and a massive wooden dragon head coming from the front. Knud opened the door and beckoned Ginny inside.

Knud's house was all one large room, made entirely of red, fresh-smelling wood, every inch of which was intricately carved with small dragon heads, spirals, gargoyles. At one end of the room, there was a large futon bed with a frame made of thick, unfinished branches. The majority of the space was taken up by a wooden worktable with carving tools and bits of ironwork. A small space was devoted to a kitchen. This was where Knud headed, removing several plastic containers from the tiny refrigerator.

"You are hungry!" he said. "I'll make you some good Danish food. You'll see. Sit down."

Ginny took a seat at the table. He began opening the containers, which were filled with a dozen or more kinds of fish. Pink fish. White fish. Fish with little green herbal specs on it. He took out some dark bread and piled these things onto a slice.

"Good stuff!" he said. "All organic, of course! All fresh! We take care of the earth here! You like smoked herring? You will. Of course you will!"

He set the heavy, fishy sandwich down in front of Ginny.

"I work in iron," Knud said. "Though I have also done some of these wood carvings. All of my work is based on traditional Danish art. I am a Viking! Eat!"

She tried to pick up the overloaded piece of bread.

"Now," he said, "you are probably wondering how I know your aunt. Yes, Peg was here, three years ago now, I think. At the arts festival. I liked her very much. She had a great spirit. One day she said to me . . . What time is it? Five o'clock?"

Somehow, Ginny didn't think that was Aunt Peg's big proclamation in Denmark.

Knud gestured for her to continue eating and then stepped out of a small doorway by his two-burner stove. Ginny ate her sandwich and looked across the canal at the row of stores on the other side. Then she turned her attention to a metal plate that sat on the table. Knud was etching it with a complicated pattern. It was amazing that such a big guy could do such delicate work.

When she looked up again, the stores she had been looking at a moment before were gone and had been replaced by a church, and even that was drifting away. The floor rocked gently underneath her, and her brain managed to put together the fact that the entire house was moving. She went to the window and saw that they had left their place at the boat sidewalk and were quickly moving through the canal.

Knud swung open the little door at the front. She could see that he was standing in a tiny booth where the boat's controls were.

"How do you like the fish?" he yelled in.

"It's . . . good! Where are we going?"

"North! You should relax! We will be some time!"

He shut the door.

Ginny opened the door that had just led from a sidewalk and found only a foot of deck and a calf-high rail separating her from the churning water. Water splashed her legs. Knud was driving his house quickly now, as they'd made it to a wider body of water. They passed under a massive bridge. At the front of the boat, Ginny looked out at the silvery channel of water that separated Denmark from Sweden.

So, she was going north. In a house.

"I live alone," Knud said, "and I work alone, but I am never truly alone. I do my ancestors' work. I live the entire history of my country and people."

They'd been sailing for at least two hours, maybe more. Knud had finally docked his house at a utilitarian pier along a road, next to a field of skinny high-tech windmills. He was a folk artist, Ginny had learned. He studied and revived crafts that were over a thousand years old, using only authentic materials and processes and sometimes getting authentically ancient injuries in the process.

What he had not explained was why he had just driven her so far north in his houseboat so that they could park along a highway. In lieu of an explanation, he made some more sandwiches, once again impressing on her the quality and freshness of all the ingredients. They sat next to the houseboat, eating these.

"Peg," he said, "I heard she died."

Ginny nodded and watched the windmills furiously spinning. They looked like mad, overgrown metal daisies. A bright orange sun gleamed behind them, shooting sharp and silvery beams off the blades.

"I am sorry to hear this," he said, landing a heavy hand on her shoulder. "She was very special. And this is why you are here, am I right?"

"She asked me to come and visit you."

"I am glad. And I think I know why. Yes. I think I do."

He pointed at the windmills.

"You see this? This is art! Beautiful. Also useful. Art can be useful. This harnesses the air and makes beautiful clean power."

They both watched the windmills spin for a few moments.

"You've come at a special time, Virginia. This is no accident. It is almost midsummer eve. Look. Look at my watch."

He held his wrist in front of her, revealing what most people would have considered to be a wall clock on a strap.

"Do you see? It is almost eleven o'clock at night. And look. Look at the sun. Peg came here for the sun. She told me this."

"How did you know her?" Ginny asked.

"She was staying with a friend of mine in a place called Christiana. Christiana is an art colony in Copenhagen."

"Was she here long?"

"No so long, I don't think," he said. "She had come to see the midnight sun. She had come to see what an extreme place this is. You see, we spend much of the year in darkness, Virginia. And then we are bathed in light, constant light. The sun bounces in the sky but never goes down. She wanted very, very much to see this. So I took her here."

"Why here?" Ginny asked.

"To see where we grow our windmills, of course!" He laughed. "She of course loved them. She saw in all of this a fantastic landscape. You come here, you understand that the world is not such a bad place. In this, we try for a better future where we do not pollute. We bathe in light. We make the fields beautiful."

They sat there for quite a while, looking at the sun that refused to go down. Finally, Knud suggested that Ginny go back into the boat and rest. She thought the light and the strangeness of the place would keep her awake, but soon the boat's gentle rocking had gotten to her. The next thing she knew, a huge hand was shaking her shoulder.

"Virginia," Knud was saying. "I am sorry. But I must go soon."

Ginny sat bolt upright. It was morning, and they were

docked back in Copenhagen, right where they had started. A few minutes after that, she was watching Knud get onto his motorcycle.

"You'll get there, Virginia," he said, resting a hand on her shoulder. "And now, I must go. Good luck."

With that, she was on the streets of Copenhagen, once again on her own.

Hippo's

At least she was prepared this time.

In case she was faced with another Amsterdam, Ginny had looked up some places online. The number-one recommended hostel on all the websites was a place called Hippo's Beach. It got five backpacks, five bathtubs, five party hats, and two thumbs up from the most thorough of the sites, which pretty much qualified it as the Ritz of youth accommodations.

Hippo's didn't look that large—just a pale gray, unassuming building with a few umbrella-shaded tables out front. The only thing unusual about it was the large model pink hippo head rearing out from above the doorway, mouth wide open. People had filled the mouth with all kinds of objects—empty beer bottles, a mostly deflated beach ball, a Canadian flag, a baseball cap, a small plastic shark.

The lobby was decorated in paper palm trees and silk garlands of flowers. There was a fake tiki bar covering wrapped around the front desk. All of the furniture was very eighties, brightly colored with geometrical patterns. There were strings of Chinese paper lanterns strung around the room.

The man behind the desk had a thick white beard and wore a bright orange Hawaiian shirt.

"Do you have any beds available?" she asked.

"Ah!" he said. "Pretty girl with pretzel hair. Welcome to the best hostel in all of Denmark. Everyone loves it here. You will love it here. Isn't that right?"

He addressed his last words to a group of four people who had just walked in with grocery bags. There were two blond guys, a girl with short brown hair, and an Indian guy. They nodded and smiled as they threw bags of hard rolls and packages of sliced meats and cheeses onto one of the tables.

"This one is a firecracker," he said. "I can see that. Look at the braids. I'll put her with you. You can keep watch for me. But here. One bunk for one week is nine hundred and twenty-four kroner."

Ginny froze. She had no idea what a kroner was or how she was going to get nine hundred and twenty-four of them.

"I only have euros," she said.

"This is Denmark!" he bellowed. "We use kroner here. But I will take euros if I must. One hundred sixty, please."

Ginny guiltily handed over the wrong currency. While she did this, Hippo reached under the bar and opened up a small refrigerator. He produced a bottle of Budweiser, which he presented to Ginny in exchange for the money.

"At Hippo's, everyone gets a cold beer. Here is yours. Sit down and drink it."

It was friendly enough, but Hippo didn't seem to expect anything but total compliance with his hospitality. Ginny took the beer uncertainly (even though she was beginning to understand that sharing alcohol was the universal way of saying "hello" in Europe). The bottle was very wet, and the label disintegrated at her touch and stuck to her palm. The people at the table, her new roommates, waved her over and offered to share their purchases.

"I just came from Amsterdam," she said, digging into her bag to try to make some kind of offering. "I have all these cookies, if you want some."

The girl's eyes lit up.

"Stroopwaffle?" she asked.

"Yeah," Ginny said. "Stroopwaffle. Eat them all. I've had too many."

She set the package on the table. Four pairs of eyes gazed at it reverently.

"She is a messenger," one of the blond guys said. "She is one of the chosen ones."

In the introductions, she learned that the two blond guys were named Emmett and Bennett. Bennett and Emmett were brothers and looked almost exactly alike—sun-bleached hair and equally faded blue eyes. Emmett dressed like a surfer, but Bennett wore an un-ironed button-down shirt. Carrie was about Ginny's height, with short brown hair. Nigel was Indian-English-Australian. They were all students from Melbourne, Australia, and they had been touring through Europe with rail passes for five weeks.

After eating, they took Ginny up to their dorm room, which was equally brightly colored—yellow walls with electric pink and purple circles along the top, blue carpet, and bunk beds made of sleek, tubular red metal.

"1983 style," Bennett said.

It was cheerful, though, and obviously well kept. They explained that everyone was supposed to help clean as part of the hostel agreement, so for fifteen minutes every day, everyone had a task. There was a clipboard out in the hallway listing jobs, so whoever got up first got the easiest, but none of them were very hard. Hippo had no curfews or kick-out times. Plus, there was a man-made beach in the back that butted up to the water.

Once again, Ginny found herself thrust into a group. But one thing was clear from the start—these were not the Knapps. Their policy seemed to be this: they got up when they felt like it, and they had no idea how long they were staying. Every night, they went out. They were thinking of leaving Copenhagen soon, but they weren't sure where they were going next. Tonight, they had very special going-out plans that Ginny had to be a part of. But first, they had to nap and eat more Stroopwaffle and give Ginny a nickname, which was Pretzels.

Ginny could live with that. She climbed into her bunk, dropped down on the thin mattress, and fell asleep.

The Magical Kingdom

There was a lot of excitement in the room when Ginny woke up.

"Here we go!" Emmett said, clapping and rubbing his hands together.

"Don't ask," Carrie said, rolling her eyes. "It's a long story. Come on. There's someplace ridiculous these morons want to go."

Again, there was no night. The sun hung steadily in the sky, only condescending to drop to a twilight level but never disappearing from view.

Copenhagen, her new friends explained to her as they walked, was the Disneyland of beer. And wherever they were going tonight was Copenhagen's Magic Mountain.

They wound up in a huge, open hall. They found seats at one of the long picnic-style tables, and Emmett signaled to one of the women that they wanted five of what she was carrying. The woman set five of the massive glass steins down on the table. Carrie passed one down to Ginny, who had to pick hers up with both hands. She sniffed at it, then took a sip. She didn't like beer that much, but this tasted pretty good. The others happily tore into theirs.

Everything was fine for about half an hour, despite the fact that she seemed to be living a poster from her school's German room—which made no sense, considering that she was in Denmark. And she was pretty sure they were supposed to be different.

Suddenly, some lights came on at the back, and Ginny became aware of a stage at one end of the room. A man in a sparkling purple jacket came up to a microphone and spoke in Danish for a few minutes. This seemed to get everyone very excited, except for Ginny, who was totally baffled.

"And now," the man said in English, "we need a few volunteers."

All at once, Ginny's four new friends exploded out of their seats, jumping up and down in a frenzy. This galvanized the Japanese businessmen who shared their table. They too sprang to their feet and started yelling and calling. Ginny, who was the only person sitting, looked down and saw dozens of empty mugs littering their half of the table.

The bandleader couldn't help but notice the international near-riot that was breaking out in their corner, and he grandly pointed to them.

"Two people, please!" he said.

It was immediately decided, through some nodding between the two parties, that since the whole table had made an effort, each group would be able to send one person. The Japanese men fell into a serious discussion, and Ginny's friends did the same. Ginny caught bits of the conversation.

"You go."

"No, you."

"It was your idea."

"Wait," Carrie said. "Let's send Pretzels."

Ginny's head shot up at that one.

"For what?" she asked.

Bennett smiled.

"Full contact karaoke," he said.

"What?"

"Come on!" Emmett yelled. "Pretzels . . . Pretzels . . . Pretzels . . ."

The other three picked up on the chant. Then the Japanese businessmen, who had already selected their representative, joined in. A few people from other tables chimed in as well, and in a matter of seconds, the whole corner of the room was calling her name. All in different accents, all loudly, all in a steady, thumping time.

Without really meaning to, Ginny found herself getting up.

"Um," she said nervously. "I don't really . . ."

"Brilliant!" Emmett shouted, helping her into the aisle between the tables. One of the Japanese men peeled off his suit jacket and joined her.

"Ito," the man said. At least, that's what Ginny thought he said. He was slurring in Japanese, so it was a little hard to tell. Ito stepped aside so Ginny could go first, even though she didn't really want to lead. The host was waving her up, and the crowd clapped its approval as she progressed toward the stage. Ito looked delighted, loosening his tie and bouncing around, waving to the crowd to keep up the applause. Ginny quietly accepted the host's hand to mount the stage. She tried to stand off in a corner, but he led her firmly to the edge, where Ito held her in place by clapping an arm over her shoulders.

The host was yelling in Danish at the crowd. The only word Ginny could make out was "Abba." He produced (seemingly from his pocket) two wigs—one a shaggy man's wig and one long and blond. The long blond one was dropped onto Ginny's head, while Ito had grabbed the other and was pulling it on crookedly. A black boa was thrown over from the direction of the bar. Ito grabbed for this first, but the host wrestled it from him and placed it over Ginny's shoulders.

The room got darker. Ginny couldn't tell if the lights were actually dropping or if this was just because the heavy blond bangs of the wig were shading her eyes. Her braids stuck out of the front, like mutant hair tentacles. She quickly tried to shove them under the lump in the back.

"How about some 'Dancing Queen'?" the host screamed, this time, in English. "How about some 'Mamma Mia'?"

The crowd liked that idea, and no group in the crowd liked it more than the Australian-Japanese contingency that had sent Ginny here in the first place. Monitors along the edge of the stage came to life. Pictures of mountain scenes and strolling couples rolled by.

And then she heard the first chord. That was when it all hit her.

They were going to make her sing.

Ginny did not sing. She especially did not sing after spending five days with the Knapps. She did not sing, ever. She did not get on stages.

Ito went first, grabbing clumsily at the microphone. Though he was smiling, Ginny sensed a genuine competitiveness—he

248

wanted this. The crowd urged him on, banging on the floor and clapping. Ginny kept trying to retreat into the background, but the host kept moving her forward. This was the last place she wanted to be. She was not doing this. She was not.

And yet, here she was, on a stage in Copenhagen under six pounds of synthetic blond hair. She *was* doing it even as her brain tried to convince her otherwise. In fact, she was in front of the microphone now, and hundreds of expectant faces were looking up at her. And then she heard the noise.

She was singing.

The really astonishing thing was, as she heard her own voice echoing around the huge bar, it almost sounded right. It was a little agonized, maybe. She kept going until she ran out of breath, closing her eyes, letting it all go in one continuous shot until her voice broke.

"Now, we will vote for the winner!"

This man screamed everything. Maybe screaming was a Danish thing.

He took Ito's arm and held it up, then nodded to the crowd to make their feelings known. There was a good amount of cheering. Then he reached over and pulled Ginny's arm up.

She was hailed like a queen when she returned to the table, Ito bowing at her the entire way. The Japanese men were obviously traveling on some kind of unlimited expense account, and they made it clear that they were paying for everyone in the group. They immediately flooded the table with various sandwiches. The beer was nonstop. Ginny made it through about a fourth of her cup. Carrie got down two entire mugs. Emmett, Bennett, and Nigel all managed to drink three each. Why they didn't die immediately was unclear to Ginny. In fact, they seemed totally fine.

By two in the morning, their new benefactors were showing the first signs of an impending collective coma. A credit card was produced, and within minutes, they were all shuffling out onto the street. After some goodbyes and thank-yous and a lot of bowing, Ginny and the Australians started heading toward the metro but were stopped by one of the Japanese men.

"No, no," he slurred, shaking his head heavily. "Tax-i. Tax-i."

He reached into his suit pocket and produced a fistful of carefully folded euros. He pressed these into Ginny's hand. Ginny tried to give them back, but the man showed a fierce determination. It was like a reverse mugging, and Ginny felt that it was best to just comply. The other men waved for taxis, and soon a little row of cars was lined up. Ginny and the Australians were ushered into an oversized blue Volvo. Nigel got into the front, and Emmett, Bennett, Ginny, and Carrie sandwiched into the broad leather backseat.

"I know where we live," Emmett said, leaning against the door with a thoughtful look on his face. "I just don't know how to get there."

Nigel said something to the driver in halting, Australian-sounding Danish that he read from a book. The driver turned around and replied, "Circle drive? What are you talking about? Do you need me to drive around? Is that what you are trying to say?"

Carrie put her head on Ginny's shoulder and nodded off to sleep.

Bennett decided to navigate from his vantage point, squashed in the middle of the backseat, barely able to see out of any window.

Whenever he managed to catch a glimpse of anything he thought he recognized, he would tell the driver to turn. Unfortunately, Bennett seemed to recognize everything. The pharmacy. The bar. The little shop with the flowers in the window. The big church. The blue sign. The driver put up with this for about half an hour and then finally pulled over and said, "Tell me where you are staying."

"Hippo's Beach," Bennett said.

"Hippo's? I know this place. Of course I know this place. You should have told me."

He pulled back on the road and turned in the opposite direction, driving quickly.

"It's starting to look familiar now," Bennett said, yawning wildly.

They were there in less than five minutes. The ride came to four hundred kroner. Ginny wasn't sure how much money she had in her hand. Whatever it was, it had been given to them for taxi fare, and this driver had put up with a lot.

"Here," she said, handing it all over. "It's all for you."

She saw him count it out as Carrie made her sleepy way out of the car. He turned and gave her a wide smile. She got the feeling that she had just given him his best tip of the year.

Hippo was still awake when they came stumbling in. He was playing Risk at one of the tables with two very intent-looking guys.

"See?" he said with a smile. "The one with the pretzels. I told you she was trouble."

#11

Dear Ginny,

I've never had a good memory for quotes. I've always tried to remember them, but it never works out. Like recently, I saw a quote by the Zen master Lao-tzu. It goes: "A footprint is made by a shoe, but it is not the shoe itself."

Fourteen words. You'd think I could remember something like that. I tried. It lasted for about four minutes, and pretty soon it was, "No shoe should be judged by its footprint, for the foot has a print of its own."

That's how it stuck in my head. And that, I thought, has no meaning. At all.

Except in your case, Gin. It may actually work for you. Because what I've done to you (or what you've chosen to do--you are your own woman) is follow in my footsteps on this insane journey I took. You're in my shoes, but the feet are yours. I don't know where they'll lead you.

Does that make any sense? It did when I thought of it. I thought you'd think I was really smart.

I ask because what I want you to do next is retrace a journey I took when I left Copenhagen. I left because the festival was over, and I had no idea what to do with myself.

Sometimes, Gin, life leaves you without
directions, without guideposts or signs. When this
happens, you just have to pick a direction and run
like hell. Since you can't get much more north than
Scandinavia, I decided to go south. And I just kept
going.

I went by train to the coast in a misty fog, then
got on a train in Germany and rode down. Down
through the mountains, down into the Black Forest.
I got off in several cities, but each time I
couldn't get any farther than the station door, and
I would just turn around and get on another
southbound train. Then I hit Italy and turned
toward the sea. I had a bright idea--I thought,
I'll go to Venice and drown my sorrows. But there
was a garbagemen's strike in Venice, so it smelled
like stinky fish--and it was raining. So I went to
the water's edge and thought, What now? Do I turn
left and go through Slovenia, maybe escape to
Hungary and eat Hungarian pastries until I
explode?

But then I saw the boat, and I just got on.

There's nothing quite like a long, slow boat ride
to clear your thoughts, Gin. A good, slow ferry
that takes its time and leaves you baking in the
sun off the coast of Italy. I was on that boat for

twenty-four hours, sitting by myself in a sticky
deck chair, thinking about all that I'd done in the
last few months. And around the twenty-third hour,
as we were coming through the Greek isles, it all
broke open for me, Gin. I saw it all clearly. I saw
it as clearly as the island of Corfu, which was
looming in front of us. I saw that I'd seen my
destination a while back, and I'd forgotten to stop.
My future was behind me.

So try it yourself, Gin. Leave now. And I mean,
now. As soon as you get this letter. Go right to the
train. Go south relentlessly. Follow the yellow
brick road all the way to Greece, to the warm
waters, to the birthplace of art, philosophy, and
yogurt.

When you get on the boat, give me a shout.

Love,
Your Runaway Aunt

P.S. Oh. Go to the grocery store first. Pack snacks.
This is a good rule to follow in all aspects of life.

The Blue Envelope Gang

It was noon the next day, and they were all recovering on Hippo's beach. Ginny sat in the cold, shallow sand and felt the wooden boards that supported the beach just under her fingertips. The sky was mostly gray, and the buildings around them were Danish canal houses and seven-hundred-year-old countinghouses, but everyone was acting like it was spring break in Palm Beach. People were sleeping on the sand in bathing suits and a large group was playing volleyball.

She scooped up some of the sand in the empty eleventh envelope, slid the letter back in, and absently folded the flap closed.

Ginny turned to her companions and said, "I've got to go to Greece. Someplace called Corfu. And I have to go right now."

Emmett looked over.

"Why do you *have* to go to Greece?" he asked. "And why now?"

It was a reasonable enough question, and the asking had attracted the attention of the others.

"I have these letters," she said, holding up the sand-filled envelope. "They're from my aunt. It's kind of a game. She sent me here. The letters tell me where I have to go and what I have to do, and when I'm done, I can open the next one."

"You're kidding," Carrie said. "Your aunt is ace! Where is she? At home or here?"

"She's . . . gone. I mean, she died. But that's okay. I mean . . ."

She shrugged to try to show them that she was all right with the question.

"So," Bennett said, "are there a lot of these letters?"

"Thirteen. This is number eleven. Almost to the end."

"And you don't know where you're going or what you have to do until you open them?"

"Nope."

The effect was kind of remarkable and seemed to solidify in the Australians' minds the idea that Ginny was a very special being. This was a very foreign feeling, and not a bad one.

"Well," Carrie said, "can we go?"

"Go?"

"To Greece. With you?"

"You want to come with me?"

"Greece sounds good. We're done here, anyway. We could use some sun. We have rail passes. Why not?"

And so, the matter was decided. Ten minutes later, they were shaking the sand off themselves and back onto Hippo's little beach and heading inside to get their things. In twenty minutes, they were online in Hippo's lounge, booking seats on a train.

Because Bennett, Emmett, Nigel, and Carrie all had Eurail passes, their route to Greece was restricted to certain trains at certain times. And because there were four of them and one of Ginny, their needs came first. Their route would take them through Germany, through Austria for a short while, then they would cut into Italy, finally stopping at Venice. It would take twenty-five hours.

Within a half hour, they were in a Copenhagen supermarket, filling a basket with fruit, bottled water, tiny cheeses sealed in wax, cookies . . . anything they could think of that might sustain them for twenty-five hours on board a train. And one and a half hours later, they were leaving Copenhagen for another Danish city called Rødbyhavn, which Ginny wasn't even going to try to pronounce. It seemed to consist only of the ferry terminal, a big, windy building. There they caught a small ferry to Puttgarden, Germany, which took about three minutes. In Puttgarden, they stood on a lonely train platform, where a sleek-looking train stopped and accepted them. They squished into a set of seats meant for four people.

As Ginny saw it, Germany was a Pizza Hut in Hamburg where she burned the roof of her mouth from eating too fast. She and Carrie got lost trying to find the women's bathroom in Frankfurt. Nigel accidentally knocked over an elderly woman as he ran for the train in Munich.

The rest was just train. In her dazed state, she remembered looking out of a window at a bright blue sky against gray mountains with white peaks soaring in the distance. Then there were miles and miles of green and fields of long, slender grasses and purple flowers. Three sudden rainstorms. Gas stations.

Colorful cottages that looked like something out of *The Sound of Music*. Rows of plain brown houses.

After the twelfth hour, Ginny began to suspect that if she sat like this much longer, hunched over with Carrie's jacket behind her head, she would be shrimp-shaped the rest of her life. Somewhere in what Ginny guessed was the north of Italy, the air conditioner died. A valiant attempt was made to open their windows, but to no avail. It didn't take long before the heat began to collect in the car, and a light but definitely funky smell hung in the still air. The train got slower. Some announcements were made about a strike somewhere. Patience was requested. The funk got funkier.

They stopped entirely for half an hour, and when they started again, the conductor asked that nobody use the bathroom.

They arrived at Venice with only fifteen minutes to spare and no idea where they were. They took their cues from the signs, trying to find the exit. Once out on the street, they piled into a small, unmarked cab, and then they were speeding down the empty streets at what felt like a hundred fifty miles an hour. A strong ocean breeze came in through the open windows as they flew, buffeting Ginny's face and causing her eyes to tear up.

And in another moment, they were all getting on a big red boat.

They were deck passengers. That meant they could sit in a chair in the lounge (already full), a chair on the deck (all taken), or the deck itself. And most of that space had been claimed. They had to walk around the boat twice before they found a narrow slice of deck between a lifeboat and a wall. Ginny stretched out as far as she could, grateful to be in the open air.

She woke up feeling a midday sun hanging right above her eyes. The heat penetrated her eyelids. She could feel an uneven sunburn on her face. She got up and stretched, then walked to the side of the boat.

The boat they were on was part of the "super-speed" line, but it didn't live up to its name. They slugged through the water at a slow enough pace to allow seabirds to land on the deck, rest, and then take off again. The water under them was a crayon-bright turquoise—the kind of color she'd never believed water could be. Ginny pulled the remaining envelopes from her bag and held them tightly (not that anything moved much—there was almost no breeze). Now the rubber band was irrelevant. It hung slack over the last two. Ginny slipped out the twelfth envelope and wound the band around her wrist.

The picture on twelve had always puzzled her. It sort of looked like the back of a purple dragon rising from the bottom edge of the envelope. Now that she was on the water, she understood exactly what it was supposed to be—it was an island. Granted, a strange picture of an island, somewhat blurry and completely the wrong color. But it was an island nonetheless.

She broke the seal and opened it.

#12

Ginny,

Harrods is the kind of thing I think you only
find in England. It's in a beautiful old building.
It's traditional. It's bizarrely organized and more
or less impossible to find anything--but if you
look hard enough, everything in the world is in
there.

Including Richard Murphy.

See, Gin, when I first arrived in London, I was
still on my adrenaline rush. But after a few days,
I realized that I was homeless, jobless, and
broke--which is a really bad combination.

You know me . . . when the chips are down, I like
to go try on fabulous, expensive things. So I went
to Harrods. I spent an entire day having makeup
put on me in the cosmetics department, trying on
dresses that cost thousands of pounds, sampling
perfume. After about eight hours of this, it
finally dawned on me that I was a grown woman
wandering aimlessly around a store like a little
kid. A little kid who had run away from home in a
snit. I had done a serious, potentially disastrous
thing.

I was down in the food hall by that point. I saw
a tall guy in a suit loading a basket with about

fifty containers of incredibly expensive African honey. I wondered to myself, Who does that? So I asked him. And he told me that he was putting together Sting's holiday baskets. I made some terrible joke about honey and stinging, and then . . . then I started crying. Crying over my whole stupid life and my situation and Sting's African honey.

Needless to say, I startled the guy. But he reacted well and sat me down and asked me what was wrong. And I explained that I was a lost, homeless American yo-yo. As it turned out, he had a spare room that he was about to place an ad to rent. He offered to cut me a deal--I could stay there for free until I had some money.

Since you aren't stupid, I know that you have already realized this guy was Richard. I moved into his spare room that day.

Now, I bet I know what you're thinking right now. You're thinking: Well, duh, Aunt Peg. What guy isn't going to take advantage of some moron woman pulling a damsel in distress? And that's a good question. Admittedly, I was taking a risk. But there was something about Richard that I trusted from the moment I met him. Richard is not exactly like the usual gang of delightful idiots I tend to spend my time with. Richard is practical. Richard likes to have a steady job and a steady life. Richard does not really understand why wall paint comes in any color aside from white. Richard is reliable. Richard never charged me a dime of rent, either.

It wasn't long before I had a serious crush going on. And though he tried to be subtle, I knew he liked me, too. And then, after a while, I realized that I loved him.

We lived with this happy arrangement for a few months. We never acted on it. It was always just there, under the surface, in the way we passed each other the remote control or said things like, "Is that the phone?" I told him I'd always dreamed of having an attic studio in Europe, and do you know what he did? He managed to find an old storage room on one of the uppermost floors of Harrods. He snuck me in every day so I could paint and I kept all my work in a cabinet there.

Then one night, he did the worst thing possible--he told me how he felt.

Now, some people--nice, normal, sane people-- might be thrilled to know that the great guy that they are in love with loves them back. Because I am not one of these people, I reacted somewhat badly.

While he was at work one day, I packed up my things and left. I was gone for months on the route that you just followed. But when I knew something was wrong with me, it was Richard I went back to. It was Richard who took care of me. It's Richard who brings me cans of Coke and ice cream while I sit and write these letters. He makes sure I take my medication at the right times because sometimes I get a little confused.

Only one more envelope to go, Gin. There is a very important task contained in that envelope--the most critical one of all. Because it is so big and serious, I am leaving it entirely up to you when you decide to open it and take it on.

Love,
Your Runaway Aunt

P.S. Do not go around taking up the offers of strange men who ask you to come live with them. That is not the moral of this story. Besides, your mom would never forgive me.

The Red Scooter

While Carrie was eagerly poring over the twelfth letter, Ginny held the thirteenth blue envelope up to the Greek sun. (Was it Greek? Was it Italian? Did anyone own it?) She couldn't see much through it. It wasn't much larger than any of the others. Felt like two pages. And this one's drawing was hardly even a drawing—it was the number 13, made to look like oversized typewritten numbers.

"Well?" Carrie asked, folding up the letter she was reading. "So you're going to open it now, right? It says you can."

Ginny sat back down and leaned back, immediately knocking her head into an oar on the side of the lifeboat behind her.

"And you *obviously* want to open it now, right?" Carrie went on. "Right?"

Ginny fished into the grocery bag. The only thing she could find in there that seemed good was one of the little cheeses. She had to nibble her way through the red wax, and by the time she got to the cheesy goodness, her mouth tasted like warm candle and she wasn't hungry anymore. She set it aside. One of the guys would eat it.

"Are fried onion blossoms a real Australian food?" she asked.

Carrie hopped up and sat down on Ginny's knees, pushing the grocery bag aside in the process.

"Oh, come on! Open it!"

"I don't get it," Ginny said. "In the beginning, it kind of made sense. Then it all got kind of random. The one guy I was supposed to meet in Amsterdam wasn't even there. Then she sent me all the way to Denmark for no reason at all."

"There had to be a reason," Carrie said.

"I don't know. My aunt was kind of crazy sometimes. She liked to see what she could get people to do."

"Well, you can solve a lot of questions by opening the last one and *reading it*."

"I know."

There was going to be something in this last letter. Something she didn't want to know. She could feel it through the paper. This letter held a lot.

"I'll open it when we get there," she said, pushing Carrie gently off her knees. "I promise."

Ginny's body had adjusted to movement, so when she realized the boat had stopped moving several hours later, she found it a little hard to walk. She swayed a little and bumped into Bennett. They joined the long line of groggy, equally confused fellow passengers, and soon they found themselves on land just before dawn.

272

The port was a dismal bunch of concrete buildings. Again, having no real idea where they were, they took a cab waiting by the port office. Emmett spoke to the driver for a moment and then waved everyone in.

"Where're we going?" Carrie asked.

"Not a clue," he said. "I said we wanted to go somewhere around here with a good beach, and we can't pay more than three euros each."

At first, the land around the road looked scrubby and hard, full of rocks and tough little plants that thrived in intense heat and gravel beds. Then the car turned, and they were on a high road above a vast beach. In front of them was a small town, just waking. Chairs were being put out in front of cafés. Ginny could see fishing boats moving in the distance.

The driver let them off along the road, pointing to a a set of steps that had been carved out of the side of the cliff that faced the water. The sand below was white, and the beach was empty. They made their way down these broad steps, clutching the rocky wall. As soon as they reached the beach, the guys immediately dropped down on the sand and stretched out to sleep. Carrie cocked an eyebrow at Ginny.

"I'll open it in a few minutes," Ginny said. "I want to walk around first."

They left their bags there and climbed over a large rock and found themselves in a small grotto. Carrie whipped off her shirt.

"I'm swimming," she said, her hands already working on her bra hooks.

"Naked?"

"Come on!" Carrie said. "You're in Greece. There's pretty much no one around. They're asleep."

Without waiting for Ginny to make up her mind, Carrie removed the rest of her clothes without a flicker of hesitation and headed for the water. Ginny thought it over for a moment. She needed to shave, seriously. But she did feel kind of gross, and the water looked unbelievable. Besides, her underwear looked pretty bathing suit–like. She would just keep that on. She yanked off her clothes and ran into the water.

It was warm as a bath. She dipped underwater and watched her braids float above her head, like antennae. Then she put her head above water and sat down on the ground, letting the waves come up over her. Carrie had obviously been cooped up way too long and was in and out of the surf. There was something almost toddler-like about her thrill to be naked.

When she'd been swept over by enough waves, Ginny pulled herself out of the small trench she was sinking into and made her way back to the rock. Carrie slogged her way out soon after and dropped straight down into the sand.

"I feel so classical," she said.

"What if they wake up?" Ginny asked.

"What? Them? They've been awake for two days, and they've been drinking lager all night. They'll sleep through anything."

There wasn't the need to say anything else. There was something so good about the morning that they could be silent and just drink in the sun and enjoy their own behavior. And when she was ready, she would open the last letter.

Up on the road above, Ginny saw some backpackers on a scooter zip by. Carrie lifted her head and watched them go.

"My friends who came here last year rented scooters," she said. "It's supposed to be the best way to see the islands. We should get one."

Ginny nodded. She liked the thought of having a scooter.

"I'm hungry," Carrie said. "I'm going to go get some food from my bag. Be right back."

"Going to get dressed?"

"Nope."

A few minutes later, Ginny heard Carrie's voice from the other side of the rock. Something about it sounded wrong.

"Where did you guys put it? It's not funny."

This got Ginny's attention. As she scrabbled over the rock, she saw Carrie, still naked (though she was clutching one of the towels to herself), circling around in a strange way. Kind of hysterical. Ginny slid back down and dressed quickly, then gathered up Carrie's clothes.

She had a feeling she was walking into a private joke, but the looks on all of their faces immediately told her that wasn't the case. Tears were streaming down Carrie's face, and the guys looked groggy but very grave.

Ginny noticed there were only three packs on the ground— the ones that had been under the guys' heads as they slept. Carrie's and Ginny's were nowhere in sight.

"Oh God," Carrie was saying, still doing her hysteria dance. "No. No. You *must* be joking with me."

"We'll look for them," Bennett was saying.

When it hit Ginny, she almost wanted to laugh.

The guys on the scooter. The fellow backpackers. They were thieves. They'd probably been watching them from the road, and then they'd come down and stolen the bags. And they'd watched them go.

Everything was gone. All her swampy clothes. And all of the envelopes. Including the last, unopened one. Her explanation had just zipped up the side of a Greek hill on a red scooter.

Ginny dug her toes into the sand.

"I'm going to go swim again," she said. She reached into her pocket and produced her only two remaining possessions, her passport and her Barclaycard. She had moved these there for safekeeping on one of the trains. She passed them to Emmett and walked to the water.

This time, she just left everything on as she walked back into the warm waves. She felt her shirt and shorts balloon up with water as she got deeper, and as the water pulled away, they suctioned to her body. All the early morning gray and lavender was burning off fast, and a bright blue sky blossomed above her. It was matched by the color of the sea. In fact, she could just about tell where the horizon was. She was in the water, and the water was in the sky—it was kind of like she was at the beginning and end of everything.

Nigel waded out to her after a few minutes.

"You all right?" he asked, looking concerned.

Ginny started to laugh.

The Only ATM on Corfu

It took about an hour to stop Carrie from raving and frantically pacing up and down the beach. Then they scrabbled (with a considerably lighter load) back up the steps cut into the sandy-colored rock to the road. They began walking back in what they guessed was the direction of the town. There was really nothing to indicate this, except that there seemed to be more hibiscus plants in that direction, and Emmett thought he saw something that might be a phone booth up ahead. It turned out to be a rock, but Ginny could understand how he made the mistake. It was kind of square.

The sun had pulled itself up high in the sky with surprising speed. The heat, combined with their exhaustion and Carrie's sporadic crying, made the going slow and somewhat painful. After a while, they could see massive modern hotels in the far, far distance and white churches and houses on points high above, jutting out over the water. About a mile up the road, they came to a clump of buildings. It turned out not to be Corfu Town, but a small village with a few small hotels and restaurants.

Everything was white. Blinding, hot white. All the buildings. All the walls. The stones that paved the ground had even been painted white. Only the doorways and shuttered windows stood out with sudden bursts of red or yellow or blue. They walked down a tiny path shaded on both sides by little trees that looked like someone had grabbed them by the top branches and twisted them like corkscrews. They were full of little green fruits, some of which had dropped and splattered open on the stones. Nigel cheerfully pointed out that they were olive trees, and Carrie, much less cheerfully, told him to shut up.

Ginny picked up a split olive from the ground. She had never seen an olive that looked like this—it was like a little lime, hard, with a skin. Nothing like those little green things with the red speck that you were supposed to drop in martini glasses.

Nothing was quite like it was supposed to be.

There was a sleepy little *taverna* with a few outside tables. They sank gratefully into the seats, and soon their tiny, round table was overflowing with plates of spinach pie, dishes of yogurt and honey, and cups of coffee. There was fresh juice as well, full of pulp and warm. Ginny put her passport and her bank card next to her plate. Strange. They took up almost no space at all, yet with them, she could travel all the way across Europe. They were all she really needed.

Carrie started weeping all over again when Ginny did this and reminded everyone that she no longer had these things. She had nothing at all. Without a passport, she wasn't going to be able to *get* anywhere. Not on a plane. Not on a ferry. And, she went on, her arms weren't *quite* strong enough to allow her to swim to the Greek mainland or back to Australia, for that matter.

Ginny quickly put her things back into her wet pocket and concentrated on dripping honey into the thick yogurt and swirling it in. She felt very bad for Carrie, but the situation didn't seem real. She felt slightly lobotomized (if you could be *slightly* lobotomized). It was a pleasant sensation, in any case. She listened as they speculated on how they could get Carrie out of Greece and back across the globe. The general consensus was that they'd have to get to the Australian embassy somehow, not that they knew where this was. The best guess was Athens.

Ginny stared off in the distance and saw a clothesline with small octopi hanging from it, drying in the sun. They made her think of Richard's washing machine and its strange alphabetical dial. What setting did you use to wash your octopus?

O, she guessed.

"What about you, Gin?" Bennett said, interrupting this mediation on the proper washing of sea creatures. "What do you want to do?"

Ginny looked up.

"I don't know," she said. "I guess I'd better get some cash."

It took a while to find an ATM among the souvenir shops and churches. The one she finally did locate was in a shop no bigger than a hallway that sold everything from canned chickpeas to rubbery-smelling bathing suits. The ATM was just a little stand-alone thing in the back, under some dusty disposable cameras. It looked kind of shady, but there was nowhere else to get any money.

She asked it for five hundred euros. The Greek message that appeared on the screen meant nothing to her, but the honking noise that accompanied it told her that it wasn't going to happen. She tried four hundred. It honked again. More honking for three hundred and two hundred. One-ninety? Nope: 180, 175, 160, 150, 145, 130, 110, 90, 75, 50 . . .

The machine eventually coughed up forty euros, then spat her card back at her in disgust.

There was only one thing she could think of to do.

The five-euro phone card didn't buy a lot of time, and the operators at Harrods didn't seem to understand her rush. The electronic voice kept interrupting her hold music to speak to her in Greek to tell her (she guessed) that the minutes were ticking away.

"Ginny? Where are you?"

"Corfu. In Greece."

"Greece?"

"Right. The thing is, my account's empty and I'm stuck," she said. "And this phone card is about to run out. I can't get back."

"Hold on a minute."

Classical music filled up the line. A voice came on and said something very chirpily in Greek. Again, she had to guess at the meaning. She was pretty sure the voice wasn't just welcoming her to Greece and hoping she had a pleasant stay. A series of short little beeps confirmed this. She was relieved when Richard came back on the line.

"Can you get to the airport in Corfu?"

"I guess so," she said. Then she realized it wasn't a guessing kind of thing. She was either going to get to the airport or stay on Corfu forever.

"Right. I'll call down to our travel agency and get you a ticket back to London. You'll be fine, all right? I'll take care of it."

"I'll pay you back or my parents . . ."

"Just get to the airport. We'll figure it all out later. Let's just get you home."

As Ginny set down the phone, she saw Carrie being tended to by all of her friends at a bench across the street. She looked somewhat calmer now. Ginny crossed the street and sat down with them.

"I have to get to the airport," she said. "Richard—my aunt's friend—is getting me a ticket out."

"You're going, Pretz?" Carrie asked. "Back to London?"

There were several rounds of hugs and an exchange of e-mail addresses. Then Emmett waved down a small beat-up Fiat that he correctly identified as a taxi. Just before it pulled away, Carrie came over to the window. She had started crying all over again.

"Hey, Pretz," she said, leaning in to Ginny. "Don't worry. You'll find out what it was."

Ginny smiled.

"You'll be okay, right?" she asked.

"Yeah." Carrie nodded. "Who knows. We may stay around here for a while. It's not like I can really go anywhere right now. There are worse places to be."

And after one final hand squeeze, the taxi pulled off, and Ginny found herself on the way to the Corfu airport.

The polite British Airways stewardess at the door to the plane didn't change her expression at all when Ginny came aboard her nice, clean aircraft. It was as if disheveled, stinky, empty-handed urchins always flew with her. She remained composed later on when Ginny accepted everything that she offered. Yes, she'd have a water. She'd take a soda, and a sandwich, and a cup of tea. Cookies, towelettes, nutcrackers, basketballs . . . Whatever she had in her little silver cart, Ginny was taking. Two, if she could get them.

It was dusk in London when her plane touched down at Heathrow. This time, after she walked the ten thousand miles of hallway, there was someone waiting for her at the end. Richard didn't seem to mind hugging her, even if she was filthy.

"My God," he said, pulling back and taking a good look at her. "What happened to you? Where are your things?"

"Everything got stolen."

"Everything?"

She reached into her pocket and produced her only two remaining possessions, the passport and the useless ATM card.

"Well," he said, "not to worry. As long as you're all right. We can get you some new clothes. What about the letters?"

"They got the letters too."

"Oh . . . right. Sorry to hear that." He stuck his hands in his pockets and nodded heavily. "Well, let's get you back."

The train was fairly crowded, despite the late hour. Richard and Ginny were squashed together. Ginny explained where she'd been after Rome. Now that she strung it all together, she realized how much had been packed into such a short time— just under a month. Seeing Keith in Paris. Getting stuck with the Knapps in Amsterdam. Riding in Knud's house to the north of Denmark.

"Can I ask you something?" Richard cut in as Ginny reached the end of her story.

"Sure."

"You don't have to tell me anything, you know, private, but . . . did Peg *tell* you anything?"

This wasn't nearly specific enough to be answered, and Richard seemed to realize that.

"I know we didn't get to talk much when you were here a few weeks ago," he went on. "But there's something you should know. In case you don't know. Do you know?"

"Know?"

"It seems like you don't. I was trying to think of a good time to sit down and tell you this, but I couldn't figure one out. So do you mind if I do it now?"

Ginny looked around the train car.

"No," she lied.

"I suppose she probably explained this in the end," he said, "in the one you didn't read. Your aunt and I were married. She needed medical care. Not that that was the only reason, of course. It just happened faster than it would have, perhaps. She told me not to say anything until you'd read everything that she'd written to you."

"Married?" Ginny said. "That means you're my uncle."

"Yes. That's exactly what it means."

He glanced over nervously. Ginny fixed her eyes in front of her.

She hated Aunt Peg at that moment. Hated her completely and totally. It wasn't her fault that the envelope had been stolen, but it was her fault that she was here, that Richard was forced to rescue her and explain these things that he obviously felt awkward about. It was better when it was all a mystery—when Aunt Peg had just been out there in the wild somewhere. She wasn't married. She didn't have a brain tumor. She was always on her way home.

In that second, as they pulled into Angel, Aunt Peg was gone. Really and truly gone.

"I have to go," she said, bolting out the door ahead of him. "Thanks for everything."

The Runaway Niece

The one advantage to having everything you own stolen is that travel becomes very easy.

She started walking, following the bus route down Essex Road. People were dressed for their night out or they were coming back from work. In both cases, it meant that they looked, as Richard would say, "smart." Or as she would say, "clean." They probably didn't smell of train funk and old wet clothes and they'd most likely bathed sometime in the last forty-eight hours.

But she didn't really care. She just kept walking, feeling her face set into a determined grimace. It was about half an hour before she realized that she had passed from the busy area with the brightly lit stores and pubs and restaurants to the smaller, tighter streets filled with liquor shops and off-track betting.

The route had imprinted itself in her mind. She turned down

to the street where all the houses were the same—all flat-fronted, dull-gray brick with white-rimmed windows. Halfway down the block she saw it, the red door with the diamond-shaped yellow window. The black blinds in the upstairs windows were crookedly pulled up halfway, and lights were on. As she got closer, she could hear music.

Someone was home, anyway. It couldn't be Keith. He was in Scotland. She'd only come here because this was the only other place in London she knew how to get to on foot. The only other place she knew besides Harrods, and she couldn't go *there*, obviously.

Maybe David would let her in.

She knocked. There were heavy footsteps running down the stairs inside, stomping along the hall.

It was Fiona who threw open the door. She was even tinier and blonder than the last time, like she'd been bleached and then left in the dryer too long.

"Is Keith here?" Ginny asked, already dreading the "no" that was sure to come.

"Keith!" she shrieked, before letting the door drop closed softly and stomping her way back upstairs in her heels.

He came to the door foamy lipped, a toothbrush handle sticking straight out of the side of his mouth. He pulled it out, swallowed hard, and wiped away the minty freshness with the back of his hand. It was only there for a second, but Ginny was sure there was a hint of a smile just as he drew back his hand. It flickered away as he took in the sight of her—rumpled, dirty, empty-handed.

"You're not in Scotland," she replied.

"The school mucked it up. We got up there only to find that we had nowhere to stay and half our performances were canceled. You look like you might need to sit down."

He stepped back and let her inside.

Keith's room looked like it had been hit by a freak tornado. The crates and boards that made up his old furnishings had given way to exploded boxes full of papers, bits of scripts, piles of books with titles like *The Theatre of Suffering*. Keith tucked the toothbrush behind his ear and started gathering up some of the papers on the sofa, clearing a spot.

"Did you just get back from Amsterdam? Or did you end up somewhere else?"

"I went to Denmark," she said. It seemed like it was so long ago, but it had been two, maybe three days? It was hard to tell anymore.

"How was that?" he asked. "Rotten? And how did you get tan there?"

"Oh." She looked down her arms. They were tan, actually. "Then I went to Greece."

"Well, why not? They're right next to each other, aren't they?"

She dropped onto the seat he had cleared. Nothing held this sofa up but some cheap foam, and that was so worn out that she sank almost all the way to the floor.

"What happened to you?" he said, kicking some books out of the way to make a seat for himself on the floor. "You look like you've just been airlifted out of some international tragedy."

"Someone stole my bag off the beach. This is all I have left."

All the energy that had propelled her for days across land and sea and air had been spent, with no result. And now she was empty, tired, with no direction left to go in. Nothing telling her where to go, and nothing keeping her from going.

"Can I just stay here for a while?" she asked. "Can I just sleep here?"

"Yeah," he said, his face clouding over. "Sure. You all right?"

"I'll just sleep on the floor or something," she said.

"No. Stay there."

Ginny lay back and pulled the pile of Keith's Star Wars comforter from its resting place on the back of the sofa. She closed her eyes and listened to him moving his papers around. She could tell he was watching her.

"The letters are gone," she said.

"Gone?"

"They were in the bag. They took the last one."

His brow wrinkled in appreciation of this fact. Ginny pulled the comforter over her nose. It smelled surprisingly clean and fresh. Maybe everything smelled that way when compared to her.

"When did you get back?" he asked. "And how?"

"Pretty much just now. Richard got me a plane ticket."

"Richard? Is that your aunt's friend that you've been staying with?"

"Kind of more than that," she said.

"Meaning?"

She shifted a bit deeper into the sofa.

"He's my uncle.

"You didn't say that before."

"I didn't know."

Keith sat down on the floor next to the sofa and stared at her.

"You didn't know?" he asked.

"I just found out. They were married, but just for health insurance or something, because she was sick. But they also liked each other. It's complicated. . . ."

"You just found out? Now?"

"Richard just told me. And then I kind of ran away."

She tried to bury those last few words in the fabric, but he seemed to catch them.

"What the hell is wrong with you?" he asked.

It was a good question.

"Don't," he said, pulling the blanket down. "You have to go back there."

"Why?"

"Look," he said, "this guy Richard cared enough to get you a plane ticket. He married your mad aunt because she was sick. And that is not fake. This whole thing is weird, granted, but that at least is real."

"You don't get it," she said, sitting up. "She wasn't dead before. She was just gone. I knew she was dead. They told me she was dead. But I never saw her get sick. I never saw her die. Now she's dead."

Now she had done it. Now she had said it. Now her voice was starting to crack. Ginny dug her fingers into the blanket. Keith sighed, then sat down next to her.

"Oh," he said.

Ginny clenched a fistful of Death Star.

"All right," he said. "You can sleep here, but in the morning I'm driving you back to Richard's. Deal?"

"I guess," Ginny said. She rolled over toward the back of the sofa and felt Keith's hand slowly rest on the back of her head and slowly stroke her hair as she broke into sobs.

The Green Slippers and the Lady on the Trapeze

The spare key to Richard's house was there in the crack of the stair, waiting for her. On the table, there was a note that read: *Ginny, If you're reading this, you've come back, and I'm happy about that. Please stay until this evening so that we can talk some more.*

"See?" Keith said, spying a loose piece of breakfast cereal and popping it into his mouth. "He knew you'd be back."

He drifted out of the kitchen and looked around the rest of the house, stopping at the door to Ginny's room.

"This is my . . ." Ginny began. "My . . . it was my aunt's room. I know it's a little . . ."

"You aunt painted all of this?" he said, running his hand along the trail of cartoons that decorated the wall, then stooping to look at the patchwork on the blankets. "It's bloody amazing."

"Yeah, well . . . this is what she was like."

"It looks a bit like Mari's place," he said.

He circled the room, taking in all of the details. He walked over to the Manet poster.

"This is her favorite painting?" he asked.

"She loved it," Ginny said. "She had a copy of it in her apartment in New York, too."

She'd stared at this poster so many times before . . . but like Piet, she'd never noticed much about it. Aunt Peg had explained it, but she'd never *gotten* it. Now the girl's flat expression in the midst of all the activity, all the color . . . it made a lot more sense. It was a lot more tragic. All of that activity in front of her and the girl wasn't seeing it, wasn't enjoying it.

"When you look at it," she said, "you're standing where the artist is supposed to be. The thing that she loved about it, though, was that nobody ever notices the green slippers in the corner. It's a reflection of a woman standing on a trapeze, but you can only see her feet. Aunt Peg always wondered about her. She was always talking about her green slippers. See? Right here."

Ginny stepped on the bed and poked at the upper left corner, where the little green slippers dangled their way into the picture. As she touched the poster, she felt a lump under the corner, right where the green slippers were. She ran her fingers along the surface. It was all smooth except for this point. She pulled on the corner. The poster was attached to the wall with sticky blue putty, which gave way easily when Ginny peeled it back. Under the corner, there was a larger lump of this blue stuff.

"What are you doing?" Keith asked.

"Something's under here."

292

She pulled the entire corner of the poster down. They both stared at the glop of blue putty and the small key that was pressed into it.

The key sat between them on the kitchen table. They'd tried it in all of the door locks to the house. Then they'd looked all through Ginny's room, trying to find anything that it might fit into. Nothing.

So now there was nothing to do but drink tea and stare at it.

"I should have known to look there," Ginny said, putting her chin on the table and getting a close-up view of the crumbs.

"Was there anything in any of the letters telling you to open something?"

"No."

"Did she ever give you anything else?" Keith asked, flicking the key across the table with his finger. "Besides the letters."

"Just the bank card." She reached into her pocket and set the Barclaycard on the table. "It's useless now. There's nothing left in the account."

Keith picked up the card and flicked it to the edge of the table.

"All right," he said. "What now?"

Ginny thought this one over.

"I guess I should take a bath," she said.

Richard had anticipated this need as well. Sitting on the floor by the bathroom door were some of his smaller clothes, some running pants and a rugby shirt. She soaked herself until she pruned. She hadn't had this luxury in a while—really hot water, towels, the time to actually get clean.

When she emerged, Keith was watching the tiny round window of the under-the-counter washing machine.

"Put your clothes in for a wash," he said. "They were disgusting."

Ginny always thought that the only way of getting clothes clean was by drowning them in scalding water and then whipping them around in a violent centrifugal motion that caused the entire washing machine to vibrate and the floor to shake. You beat them clean. You made them suffer. This machine used about half a cup of water and was about as violent as a toaster, plus it stopped every few minutes, as if it were exhausted from the effort of turning itself.

Sluff, sluff, sluff, sluff. Rest. Rest. Rest.

Click.

Sluff, sluff, sluff, sluff. Rest. Rest. Rest.

"Who thought to put a window on a washing machine?" Keith asked. "Does anyone just sit and watch their wash?"

"You mean, besides us?"

"Well," he said, "yeah. Is there any coffee?"

Ginny got up, tripped over the long running pants, and went to the cabinet for the jar of Harrods instant coffee. She set it on the table in front of Keith.

"Harrods," Keith said, picking up the jar.

There was a nearly-audible click in Ginny's head.

"Harrods," she repeated.

"Harrods, indeed."

"No. The key. It's for Harrods."

"Harrods?" Keith said. "You're telling me your aunt had the magical key to Harrods?"

"Maybe. Her studio was there."

"Inside *Harrods*?"

"Yes."

"Where was her bedroom? Inside Parliament? Top of Big Ben?"

"Richard works at Harrods," Ginny said. "He found her a space to work in. She kept everything in a cabinet there. A cabinet would have a small key, like this one."

Keith shook his head.

"Why does this surprise me?" he asked. "Come on, then. Let's go."

The Magical Key to Harrods

Ginny had switched off the "what am I wearing?" impulse in her brain several hours before as a means of survival. It wasn't until she caught her reflection in the window at Harrods that she suddenly remembered how she was dressed and that she was accompanied by someone wearing a shirt that said, CORPORATE SWINE ATE MY BALLS.

Keith looked equally distressed as he peered in through the door that the Harrods doorman was holding open for them.

"Cor," he said, his jaw dropping at the sight of the oozing mass of humanity that completely filled every square foot of space. "I am *not* going in there."

Ginny grabbed his arm and pulled him inside, leading him down the now-familiar path to the chocolate counter. The expression on the chocolate woman's face said that she was not impressed with either of their outfits. But it also said that she was a professional and that she had seen every kind of insane person pass through Harrods' doors.

"Just a moment," she said, "Murphy, yes?"

"How did she know that?" Keith asked as the woman walked to the phone. "How do you have all of these strange connections inside Harrods? *Who are you?*"

Ginny realized that she was biting at her cuticles. She never did that. She was suddenly very nervous about seeing Richard. Her uncle. The one she'd run from.

"My mum used to drag me here whenever we came down to London at Christmas," he went on, bending down low and scanning the contents of the chocolate counter. "It's even worse than I remember."

She had to move away from Keith, from the chocolate lady . . . and she had to fight the desire to slip into the crowd and disappear. She almost lost the battle but caught sight of Richard's short curls and his silvery tie and dark shirt coming at her through the crowd. She couldn't look up at him as he approached. Instead, she simply opened her hand and stuck it forward, revealing the tiny key that had imbedded itself in her palm.

"I found this," she said. "It was in Aunt Peg's room, behind a poster. I think she left it there for me, and I think it's for something here."

"Here?" he asked.

"The cabinet. Is it still here?"

"It's in a storage closet upstairs. But there's nothing in it. She brought her paints home."

"Could this be the key for it?"

Richard took the key and looked it over.

"It could be," he said.

Ginny snuck a quick look at him. He didn't look angry.

"Come on," he said. "I have a minute. Let's go have a look."

Aunt Peg's Harrods studio was not a glamorous place. It was a very small room on a top floor with a bunch of deformed mannequins and discarded hangers. There was a cloudy window that pushed open and revealed only gray sky.

"It's one of these," Richard said, pointing to a clump of large, brown metal cabinets in the corner.

It wasn't any of the front ones, so Keith and Richard were forced to start pushing the cabinets around so that Ginny could squeeze between the row and try the other locks. The fifth one was a perfect fit. The inside of the cabinet was completely hollow. There was plenty of room for the pile of rolled canvases at the bottom.

"The dead Harrods scrolls," Keith said.

"It's strange that she would take her paints home but leave the paintings here," Richard said. "I never would have found them. They would have been thrown away."

Ginny unrolled a few of the canvases and spread them out on the floor. The work was clearly Aunt Peg's: bright, almost cartoonish representations of now-familiar sights. There were the Vestal Virgins, the Eiffel Tower, the white-paved paths of Greece, the London streets, Harrods itself. A few were almost direct copies of the pictures on the envelopes. There was the girl at the base of the mountain under the castle from the fourth letter, the rising sea monster island from number twelve. Ginny had seen lots of amateur painters painting these sights on her travels to sell as souvenirs to tourists. These paintings were very different. They were alive. They seemed to vibrate.

"Hang on." Keith reached over and pulled off something taped to the inside of the door. He looked at it and then held it over for Ginny and Richard to see. It was a heavy, dove gray card, with a name and number darkly imprinted.

"Cecil Gage-Rathbone," Keith said. "*That's* a name."

Ginny reached for the card, then flipped it over. Scrawled in pen were the words CALL NOW.

They got the paintings, twenty-seven in all, out of the cabinet in packing tubes and oversized Harrods shopping bags. Richard had to spend a few minutes in the hallway convincing a very old security guard that they weren't actually stealing things from the storeroom and finally had to flash something he carried in his wallet. The man backed away and apologized profusely.

They made their way to his office, which was a tight space entirely occupied with file cabinets and boxes. There was barely enough room to get over to the desk to use the phone.

Cecil Gage-Rathbone had a voice like ringing crystal.

"Is this Virginia Blackstone?" he asked. "We were told you'd be contacting us. We have all the paperwork ready—we've been preparing for this for months. I think we could manage . . . *Thurs*day? Is that too soon? That only gives you two days."

"Okay," Ginny said, having no idea what he was really talking about.

"When would you like us to collect them?"

"The paintings . . . right?"

300

"Yes, that's right."

"Um . . . whenever."

"We could send someone round this evening, if that is agreeable. We'd like to get them in-house as soon as possible to prepare things."

"It's . . . agreeable."

"Excellent. Is five o'clock all right?"

"Sure?"

"Splendid. Five o'clock, then. Same address in Islington?"

"Yes?"

"Very good. You'll just need to come here at nine in the morning on Thursday. Do you have our address?"

After taking all the information from Cecil, who worked for something called Jerrlyn and Wise, Ginny set down the phone.

"Some people are coming to take the paintings," she said.

"Who?" Richard asked.

"No idea. But we have to go to this address on Thursday at nine. Or at least I do."

"For what?"

"I'm not sure."

"Well, you've sorted that, then, haven't you?" Keith said. "Mystery solved."

He looked between Richard and Ginny, then back toward the door.

"You know what?" he said. "I've been meaning to have a better look at those famous food halls. Get something for my gran."

"Sorry about . . . leaving," she said, once Keith was gone.

"Well, you're Peg's niece," he said. "It's in your blood. And it's all right."

Richard's phone began ringing. It was a very loud, insistent phone. No wonder he always sounded hassled here.

"You better get that," she said. "The queen might need underwear."

"She'll wait a moment," he said. "I'm sure she has lots of pants."

"Probably."

Ginny kept her eyes on the dull green carpet. There were little paper circles everywhere, obviously fallen from the reservoir of a hole punch. It looked like snow.

"We should really get you some clothes," he said. "Why don't you go pick out some things, and I'll have them charged to my account? Nothing too crazy, if you don't mind, but get yourself something you like."

Ginny nodded heavily. Her eyes were tracing patterns of dots on the floor. A star. A one-eared rabbit.

"I'm sorry," he said. "I shouldn't have told you on the train. I don't know what I was thinking. I *wasn't* thinking. Sometimes I just say things."

"It never seemed real," she said.

"What didn't? Peg and I? I don't know what it was, really."

"Her being gone," Ginny explained. "She sometimes did stuff like that."

"Ah."

Another, even louder line started to ring. Richard glanced over at his phone in annoyance, then depressed a few buttons, which silenced it.

"She always promised me she would be there," Ginny said. "For high school, college. She would promise things and then just not do them. And just leave without telling anyone."

"I know. She was awful like that. But she could get away with it."

It took effort, but she pulled her gaze from the floor. Richard was absently pushing a folder around his desk.

"I know," she said. "She could. She was really irritating like that."

"Very," he agreed. There was a thoughtful sadness about him—one that seemed very familiar.

"I guess she did know what she was doing, a little," she said. "I got an uncle out of it, at least."

Richard stopped pushing his folder and looked up.

"Yeah." He smiled. "It's nice to have a niece, too."

The Padded House

On Thursday morning, a black cab containing Ginny, Richard, and Keith wound its way down a quiet London street—the kind of quiet that whispers wealth, tradition, and the presence of lots of high-tech security systems.

Aside from being a bit bigger than the buildings around it, the Jerrlyn and Wise building had nothing to suggest that it was anything other than a house. The only thing identifying it was a tiny brass plate by the front door, which was swung open immediately by a man with frighteningly perfect blond hair.

"Miss Blackstone," he said. "You look *so* much like your aunt. Please, *do* come in. I'm Cecil Gage-Rathbone."

Cecil Gage-Rathbone's dove gray suit matched the business card that they had found stuck to the cabinet door. His cuff links shimmered discreetly from the ends of sleeves that had to be made of obscenely high-count cotton. He *smelled* tailored.

If Keith's green Jittery Grande kilt, black shirt, and red tie threw Cecil at all, he didn't show it. He introduced himself and shook hands with genuine pleasure, as if he had waited all his life to meet Keith and was full of sweet relief now that the moment had finally come. He took Ginny gently by the shoulders and glided her along past the antiques and the handful of gathered people as well tailored and coiffed as himself.

Cecil offered them food and drinks from an impressive display of silver pots and plates arranged on a long mahogany sideboard. Ginny couldn't take anything, but Richard accepted a cup of coffee, and Keith took champagne, strawberries, tiny scones, and a huge dollop of cream. Cecil led them through a long hallway to the auction room. Everything was thick and plush—the heavy drapes on the windows, the soft, overstuffed leather chairs. It was so padded and low-key that it was hard to hear Keith's murmured monologue on how much he'd always wanted to play James Bond and was very happy to be at the audition.

They stopped at the end of the hall, at a room where even more people in suits sat and chatted quietly into cell phones. Blue chairs had been set up along the sides, along with tables that were wired up for laptops. The canvases had been put into simple glass frames and set up on easels at the front of the room.

Cecil ushered them into seats in the corner and then hovered over them, poking his head between them to speak in confidence.

"What *I* think," he whispered, "is that we're quite *like*ly to get a good offer for the col*lec*tion as a whole. People are calling them the Harrods paintings. Everyone loves a good story."

It was only now that they were spread out and lined up that

Ginny could understand what the paintings were. She looked over to Richard, who was looking at them the same way, running his eyes down the line as if reading a sentence from a book.

The images started off bright and clear and powerful, like cartoon art. The next ones were similar but done in angry, quick slashes of paint that suggested haste. Then the colors began to fade and become muddled together, and the proportions became very strange. The last ones were in many ways the most beautiful and certainly the most striking. The bright colors and strong lines were back, but the images were fantastically wrong. The Eiffel Tower split into two pieces. The London buses were fat and comical and purple, and flowers grew along the city streets.

"She was sick," Ginny said, mostly to herself.

"This work is a record of her illness, which makes it very unique," Cecil said carefully. "But you should know that your aunt's work had started to attract attention before she fell ill. She was being promoted as the next Mari Adams, who has been quite a vocal supporter of your aunt. We had a few major buyers ready and waiting for these paintings months ago."

Mari Adams . . . Lady MacStrange. From the way Cecil's voice went up just a little on saying her name, Ginny could tell that Mari really was a big deal, at least to him.

"So why didn't she sell them?" Ginny asked.

Cecil folded himself in even lower.

"You must know that she was fully aware that the collection's value would increase after her . . . passing on. That is the way of the art world. She deliberately delayed the sale."

"Until . . . afterward."

"Until I was contacted by you, but yes. That was the impression I was given."

He bent his knees and came down even farther until his head was completely level with theirs.

"I understand that this may be a bit odd for you, but everything is arranged. Your proceeds will be wired to your bank account as soon as the sale is finalized."

His attention was drawn to the buzzing of his cell phone.

"Excuse me for a moment," Cecil said, cupping his hand over his phone. "It's Japan."

Cecil retreated to the side of the room, and Ginny fixed her eyes on the back of the head of the man sitting in front of her. He had a large red blotch that the buttery comb-over of his four remaining gray hairs couldn't hide.

"We don't have to do this," Ginny said. "Do we?"

Richard didn't reply.

This room was too mute. Too cool for the weirdness that was going on in her head. She wished Keith would make a crack about the entire nation of Japan calling for Cecil or the fact that she had scrubbed the final remains of what was probably a valuable work of art off her arm just that morning. But he said nothing.

Ginny bored her eyes into the head blotch. It kind of looked like Nebraska.

"All right." Cecil was standing next to them again, clicking his phone shut. "Are you ready?"

Ginny noticed that Richard was intently keeping his eyes off the pictures. They were causing him real pain.

"I guess," Ginny said.

Cecil took his position at a stand at the front of the room. Instead of putting away their phones, the people without them suddenly pulled them out and put them to their ears. A few more laptops opened up. He gave a very prim introduction and politely started the bidding at ten thousand pounds.

For a moment, nothing happened. A gentle buzz spread around the room as this figure was repeated into the phones in a variety of languages. No one spoke out or raised a hand.

"Ten thousand at the front," Cecil said. "Thank you."

"Where?" Keith asked, his mouth half full of strawberry and cream.

"And twelve," Cecil said. "Twelve. Thank you, sir. Now at fifteen thousand."

Ginny still saw nothing, but Cecil caught these gestures through some kind of magical transference.

"Fifteen thousand from the gentleman on the right. Do I hear eighteen? Thank you very much. And twenty? Yes, sir. Very good. On to thirty?"

Keith very slowly lowered his plate to his lap and grabbed the sides of his chair.

"Did I just bid that twenty?" he whispered. "When I was eating. Do you think I . . . ?"

Ginny shushed him.

"Thirty. Very good. Thirty-five? Thank you. Forty. Forty to madam in the front . . ."

Richard hadn't lifted his head from the program that sat closed on his lap. Ginny reached over and found his hand, and she didn't stop squeezing it until the bidding stopped at seventy thousand pounds.

Seventy Thousand Burlap Sacks

The next morning, Ginny woke up feeling like she'd grown several inches. She squirmed on the bed, twisting toward the right and left, trying to determine if this was just a dream hangover or if the sudden influx of money had actually *expanded her spine.* She reached her toes down to see if she was taking up the same amount of space on the bed as she had all along. It seemed to be the same.

The money would soon be shifted from one computer to another, and then it would just appear in her bank account. Like magic. It seemed strange to her that it would come down to money. A figure. It was just a number, and you can't leave someone a *number.* That was like leaving someone an adjective or a color.

She imagined the tiny burlap pound sacks again. This time, there were seventy thousand of them. They filled up this room, stacked high against the yellow and pink walls, covering the carpet . . . covering her, going right over the top of the Manet print until they hit the ceiling.

It was a little alarming, actually.

She rolled out from under the phantom pile and slipped out of bed. She'd slept late, she noticed, and Richard had already come and gone. He'd left the newspaper spread open for her on the table, with a circle around the day's exchange rate. He'd also penciled in the margin *$133,000 US.*

The imaginary pile reappeared in her mind, and doubled. This time, it was a sea of light, loose dollars, waist high, filling the kitchen and swallowing up the table.

This couldn't be Aunt Peg's big surprise. There had to be something more, she was sure of it now. But she was going to need help figuring out what that something was, obviously. Which meant only one thing.

The television was on when she arrived, but Keith wasn't watching it. A long-haired man was opening up cans of paint for two surprised-looking people in matching shirts. Keith was bent over his notebook and didn't even look up as Ginny came in and sat down on the sofa.

"Listen to this," he said. "*Harrods: The Musical.* In a modern mythological context, the department store represents . . . what?"

She could feel that her eyes were wide and her expression was blank and frozen.

"What do you think she wants me to do with it?" she asked. "The money?"

Ginny nodded. Keith sighed and closed his notebook on his hand to hold the page.

"I don't mean to put too fine a point on it," he said, "but *she* is dead, Gin. *She* doesn't want you to do anything with it. The money is yours. You do with it what you want. And if what you want is to invest in *Harrods: The Musical*, it is not my place to stop you."

He looked over at her in anticipation.

"Worth a shot," he said. "All right, then. Why not travel?"

"I just traveled."

"You traveled some. You can always travel more."

"I don't really want to travel," she said.

"You could stay in London. Lots to do in London."

"I guess," she said.

"Look," he said with a sigh, "you've just been given loads of cash. Use it on anything you want. Stop wondering about that last letter, which must be what you're wondering about. You figured it all out. It all worked out."

She shrugged.

"What did you *want* it to say?" he asked. "You know it would have led you back to the poster. You managed to get what she was trying to give you. You found out Richard is your uncle. What more is there to know?"

"Can I ask you something?" she said.

"Apparently there *is* something you want to know."

"Are we dating?" she asked.

"What is *dating*, really?"

"Don't," she said. "Seriously."

"All right." Keith reached over and switched off the television. "It's a fair question. "But you've got to go home, eventually. You know that."

"I know," she said. "I was just checking. But are we kind of something?"

"You know how I feel."

"But," Ginny said, "can you . . . say it?"

"Yeah." He nodded. "We're definitely kind of something."

There was something in the fact that he said it—said *something*—that made Ginny incredibly happy.

And in that second, she knew exactly what it was the thirteenth envelope would have told her to do.

Lucky Thirteen

It wasn't logical, but in Ginny's mind it seemed like there should have been something special to commemorate the sale of the "Harrods paintings." But Harrods seemed unaware of the event or the artist it had been harboring in its eaves. Harrods was just Harrods. Busy, crowded. Life was moving on here as it had before. The woman at the chocolate counter rolled her eyes as Ginny approached.

"Just a moment," she said. "I'll call Mr. Murphy."

Ginny had stopped on the way to see if any money had appeared in her account. It had, in fact—so she took out a hundred pounds for good measure. She pulled it out of her pocket now and concealed it in her palm.

"He's on his way down, miss," she said unenthusiastically.

"What's the best chocolate you have?" Ginny asked, looking over the display.

"It depends on what you like."

"Which ones do you like?"

"The champagne truffles," she said. "But they're sixty pounds a box."

"I'll take one."

The woman raised her eyebrows as Ginny slid over the money. A moment later, she was presented with a heavy bronze box. Ginny tucked the receipt under the brown ribbon and slid the box back toward the woman.

"These are for you," she said. "Thanks for everything."

As she walked away from the counter, she wondered if this having money thing might not just work out after all.

She took Richard to the fancy tearoom. It seemed like the right thing to do. For all the time she'd spent in England so far, she hadn't had any fancy tea. Now they were facing down a multi-tiered tray of tiny sandwiches and cakes.

"Come to spend your fortune?" Richard asked.

"Kind of," she said. She stared down into the delicate porcelain teacup their waiter had just filled.

"What does that mean?"

"I was right to sell the paintings," she asked, "wasn't I?"

"I was there for that bit," he said. "The end, all the confusion. That's what those paintings caught. I don't want to remember that bit, Ginny. It wasn't always her."

"How did she even write the letters?" Ginny asked.

"She was lucid sometimes, and in the next moment, she'd think that the walls were covered in ladybugs or that the postbox had just spoken to her. To be honest, sometimes I couldn't tell if it was painful or if she was enjoying all the strange things she was seeing. Peg was . . . full of wonder."

"I know what you mean," Ginny said.

They filled their plates with the tiny sandwiches. Richard ate for a few minutes. Ginny assembled hers in four points along the edge of her plate like a compass, or maybe a clock.

"In the last letter I read," she began, "she told me something. It just occurred to me that she may not have told you."

Richard froze mid-reach for a tiny cucumber sandwich.

"She said she loved you," Ginny went on. "She said she was head over heels for you. She was mad at herself for leaving, but she was just frightened. But just so you know."

Judging from the look on his face (she thought his eyebrows might come loose from all the wiggling up and down), Ginny knew that he hadn't known this. And she also knew that now, she was really done. She suddenly felt very light.

In fact, she wasn't even embarrassed when Richard came over to her side of the table and wrapped his arms around her.

13

Dear Aunt Peg,

Not sure if you know this, but the thirteenth
blue envelope is gone (it was stolen along with my
bag in Greece). Anyway, I figured I'd take over.
Just so you know, Richard got me back to London,
and I figured it out. I should have realized about
the green slippers.

We made a lot of money. People really liked your
paintings. So, thanks for that.

You know, I wanted to write to you for a long
time, but I never could. You never left an address
where I could reach you, and you never did check
your e-mail. So now I'm writing to you when you're
dead, which is kind of dumb. There's nowhere I can
send this letter. I have no idea what I am going
to do with it. It's kind of ridiculous that the
only one of the famous thirteen letters I'll have
is one I wrote.

The truth is, if I had been able to write to
you, I probably would have just yelled at you. I
was mad at you. And even though you've explained
it all to me, I'm still kind of mad at you. You
went away, and you never came back. I know you
have "issues," and I know you're different and
creative and all those things, but it really

wasn't okay. Everybody missed you. My mom was worried about you--and as it turned out, she should have been.

At the same time, you pulled off this incredible trick. You got me over here, made me do all of these things that I'd never have done otherwise. And I guess even though you were telling me what to do, I still had to do them on my own. I always thought that I could only do things with you, that you made me more interesting. But I guess I was wrong. Honestly, I pulled some of this stuff out of my butt. You would have been proud. I'm still me. . . . I still find it hard to talk sometimes. I still do incredibly stupid things at inappropriate moments. But at least I know I'm capable of doing some things now.

So I guess I can't be too mad. But I can still miss you. Now that I'm here, in your room, spending your money . . . you've never seemed farther away. I guess it will just take time.

Since I won't need the blue envelope to mail this, I'm going to put half of the money in it and leave it for Richard. I know you gave it all to me, but I'm also pretty sure that you wanted him to have some of it. He is my uncle, after all.

I've also decided to do what you never managed

to do but what I know you probably wish you
did . . . I'm going to go home.

                    Love,
                    Your Interesting,
                    International Niece

P.S.
Oh, and I told him for you.

13 Little Blue Envelopes

Meet Maureen Johnson

HELLO! I'm Maureen Johnson, and I wrote this book. Here are some important facts about me that you may want to use to pad out any book reports you are writing, even ones that aren't on one of my books.

Where I was born: In Philadelphia, during a massive snowstorm, at 5:20 on a Friday morning. It was the last time I got up that early on my own accord.

Where I live: In New York City.

Current weather conditions: Extremely cold. Like, lose-a-finger cold.

Opinion of current weather conditions: I don't love the cold. I always say how lovely and sparkly New York is in the cold and how the winter is so bracing and wonderful, but I know now that I am just lying to myself and others. It is very useful, though, when you have to say, "I'm just going to stay in tonight where it's nice and snug and write."

First "real" book I remember reading: Sir Arthur Conan Doyle's *The Hound of the Baskervilles*, in a condensed version for children, probably when I was five or six.

Last book read before writing this: I had two going, which I finished around the same time. One was *The Scarlet*

EXTRAS

Pimpernel and the other was *The Pirates! In an Adventure with Scientists*. Both were quite exciting.

Books read in the Swedish language: Only one, *The Key to the Golden Firebird*, my first book, in translation. And I wasn't really reading it. I just felt like I was because I knew what it said when it was in English. It looked pretty much like Ikea catalog copy to me otherwise. I just like bringing this up because for fifteen or so minutes I actually thought I knew Swedish, and I hold on to those minutes.

Where I write: At my desk, or, if I'm not at home, the sunniest spot I can find with a nice, clean surface. I am very much against taking my computer and writing into bed, or in front of the television. I don't like to mix activities. I think it's good to have a spot for working, a spot for relaxing, and a spot for sleeping. Kitchen tables are okay, though.

What I use: A computer, currently a small silver Apple PowerBook named Gilda.

How many beverages I have while I work: A stupid number. I drink constantly. Cups and mugs litter my desk. To see my desk, you would think five people were working there. Five very thirsty people.

Current beverage count: One mug, one glass. Both empty.

Maureen on the Writing of
13 Little Blue Envelopes

13 Little Blue Envelopes was started during a one-month writers' residency I did in a castle just outside of Edinburgh, Scotland. It was February, which isn't maybe the best time of year to go to Scotland. I had the basic idea to work with before I left, but the actual writing started there.

There were five of us in the castle, along with the administrator. The housekeeper, the handyman, and the cook came during the day—otherwise, it was just us. We were surrounded by Scottish wilderness. Being from New York, all wilderness is extremely wild to me, so for the entire time I lived in fear of being eaten by badgers and owls. I did most of my work in a cold, sunny room overlooking the river and glen. I worked at a thick medieval-style table for as long as I had light. The floor of the room where I worked was covered in extremely real fur rugs which I tried never to go near—they were the only warm thing about the room. I still get a little chilly when I look at letters #2 and #3.

What the experience definitely did was force me to remember what it was like to be (basically) alone in a place that is unfamiliar and really *feels* unfamiliar. We had no Internet, no television, and very little phone time. It was profoundly quiet. At the end of the day (it

5

got dark around three in the afternoon or something), we would gather around the fire and drink sherry. It was an amazing experience, though I think I was about two inches away from madness for the first three weeks. Being cut off, not having e-mail or a cell phone, feels strange.

I think things started to turn for me on my birthday, which fell in the middle of my stay. I went to Edinburgh during the day. We could get there using a bus that ran past the castle gate, at the end of a fairly long drive that cut through the woods. Even though I left the city early, it was pitch black when I came home. The driver didn't know where the entrance to the castle drive was (as I had been told he would). It was pure luck that I spotted a building I recognized, hit the stop button, and jumped off.

So, I was on a Scottish roadside, alone, on a cold winter's night. With some effort, I managed to find my way back to the drive entrance and faced the absolute blackest, blackest pathway I have ever seen. There was no light whatsoever. I couldn't even see the ground. The castle was totally out of sight.

If you'd spent a week hearing things about all the bloody battles that were fought around the area (plenty of places to dump a body around here), the quiet (definitely one of those places where you could scream and scream and no one would hear you), the wildlife, and if you are kind of cowardly like me, you'd have thought twice about going down that dark drive as well. I could hear things scurrying. I did not want to go down that path through the woods in the dark. I wanted the castle to magically appear in front of me. I remember standing there, totally unwilling to move.

But I had no choice. What was I going to do? Stand there all night?

So I started walking into the void. I could tell I was on the path when the soles of my shoes struck something solid and smooth. If they hit something softer and crinklier, I was off of it. I made up a little song to scare away any creatures that came along. (The noise, I mean. The song itself was pretty entertaining, as I remember it.)

The feeling I had going down that path was like nothing I'd ever experienced before. It was so literal, so dark and unknown, and at the end, there was a castle, all lit up by a spotlight on the lawn. And that was the moment, really, when Ginny's experience hit me. It was going to be forced, it was going to be scary at times (even if not truly dangerous), but it was going to have a big, grand thing waiting at the end.

Later, in the castle library, I happened to pull an old *Paris Review* from the shelf. I opened it at random and found myself looking at a picture of a woman with crazy hair and tattoos all over her face. For some reason, I read the article. I became fascinated by its subject, an artist named Vali Myers. She became my inspiration for

EXTRAS

Mari Adams, Peg's mentor in Edinburgh. I took several real-life facts from Vali's life—like Mari, she really did have a cage that she locked herself in to work, she really did tattoo the names of her dead pets on her body, and at one point she gave over the ownership of her left hand to her pet fox, Foxy. I found out after I wrote the book that she even drew tattoos on other people's bodies, including one very famous female singer, just as Mari does to Ginny.

That's when it all took off, really. That was how Ginny and all of the others came together. They were all born in a castle.

A Q&A about *13 Little Blue Envelopes*

Do any elements of *13 Little Blue Envelopes* come from your own life experiences?

Well, in terms of general travel, absolutely. I can relate to both Peg and Ginny. My point of view is fairly equally split between them.

But there are plenty of things in the book that are born out of more concrete experience. For example, Richard actually lives in my friends' house in Islington. (Except that they are very neat, and the inside of the house is lovely. I just took the house in general. They haven't noticed so far.) There really is a man on the 6 train who always plays the *Godfather* theme song on the accordion. The Knapps are very closely based on a family I met on a trip, though they didn't make printed schedules (that I know of).

What's the first thing you put in your suitcase before a trip?

I am a famously bad packer. It's not for lack of trying, either. I make lists—careful, well-crafted lists—and yet right before I'm about to zip up the bag, I just lose my mind and start grabbing things. "I'll need two more skirts. I'm not sure which ones, so I'd better just bring five of them to be sure. And this Chinese robe! All my socks, all of them. And probably another pair of shoes. And this toaster . . ."

The best part is that when I get to the airport and they weigh my bag, I genuinely wonder why it's so heavy. It's like I have the memory span of a goldfish.

Why did you decide to write a story about a girl who travels alone through Europe?

The cheap answer is that it sounded like a lot of fun.

The really good answer you can refer to when writing your book report is: Adventure means risk—it wouldn't have been quite the same to have Ginny just opening thirteen letters at home, seated safely on the couch, surrounded by friends, family members, and cushions. Aunt Peg works on a big, wonderful scale. Her canvas is everywhere.

The route evolved sort of naturally. It's actually very easy to run away to London from New York City. And going to England is a good stepping-off point—it's foreign without being *too* foreign. The language is the same, and the culture is familiar. From there, the other destinations were all chosen as likely places an artist in search of herself (like Peg) would have ended up. The progression was designed to strip more and more of the familiar away from Ginny—language, company, belongings.

Basically, by the end of it, I wanted the readers to get that feeling that you can only get from doing a lot of European travel in a short time—it starts to wash over you. This was the reason for dragging her all the way south in one insane rush, and then putting her on a slow, slow boat to Greece.

Have you been to all of the places in the book?

I've been to about half of them. I've never been to Rome, Copenhagen, or Greece.

Did the book change at all as you wrote it?

It changed dramatically between what I think were drafts three and four. I always knew what the "solution" was, but there were a lot of things cluttering up the path. In the very first versions, Richard owned a pub, and Keith, David, and Fiona all lived there above it. Ginny spent months in London in the first versions, and Richard had a little baby girl. It's always kind of amazing to go back and read a first draft when the book's done—the first drafts always seem very foreign and odd to me. It's like someone else wrote them.

What's your favorite travel destination and why?

I haven't been to that many places. I've done a little traveling around the United States and Europe, but I wouldn't call myself well traveled. I tend to go to England over and over and over. So I guess it's England.

Do you know exactly what the 13th letter says?

Oh yes. But then, so does Ginny.

In the Words of Keith Dobson

There's nothing quite like getting an insider perspective on the story, so I've asked Keith Dobson, the character himself, to answer a few questions about his 13 Little Blue Envelopes *experience. And being Keith, he obliged.*

☆ ☆ ☆ ☆ ☆ ☆

Hello, fans.

I was asked to contribute to this paperback edition of *13 Little Blue Envelopes* because, I can only assume, you (the collective you) demanded to hear from me. I understand, and I respond!

I have been instructed by Ms. Johnson, author at large, that I not tell you anything about what happened after the point where the book leaves off . . . *if, in fact, anything did happen.* For all you know, we could have been immediately drawn into a wandering black hole and erased from existence. (Well, except that I am writing this now. I guess this is a bit of a giveaway.) So, here I am, and quite chuffed to be supplementing your reading experience. I am even wearing my kilt in honor of the occasion.

I have before me (*uncrumples paper, tosses away a bit of baguette crust contained within*) a list of questions to answer. Let us waste no more time.

☆ ☆ ☆ ☆ ☆ ☆

What did you think of Ginny when you first met her?

Well, aside from the fact that she had innate good taste in art, I did think she was completely insane. I mean, be fair . . . here's this Amazonian American (she's quite tall, is Ginny) literally buying every seat in the house at my shows, showing up at my front door, tossing handfuls of cash at me . . .

Looking back at that sentence, I can see that these are actually quite appealing things. Which probably explains why I was so very taken with her. And despite the fact that it took about ten years to extract two words from her mouth, once she got talking, she had no problem making her feelings known. That's my girl.

What was your reaction to hearing all of the things that happened to Ginny when you weren't around?

Ginny told me about a few of these things in London, but I didn't get the full story until I read the book. She left the Beppe incident out of her account to me, and I'm quite glad she did. I was *not* pleased about that one.

I'm quite proud of her, actually. It takes a fair amount of courage to do what she did. How she followed those rules to the end, I have no idea. I would have opened all of those envelopes five minutes after I got them. But that's what makes Ginny, Ginny, I suppose.

Do you feel bad about stealing the Godzilla from Mari's house?

The drawback to not being in control of the story is that you can't leave out the unflattering bits about yourself. In short, yes. Yes, I do. But I promise that I never thought she would even miss it. It was a *joke*. Mari clearly didn't mind. After the book came out, she sent me a wind-up Godzilla of my very own, along with a box of chocolates. I submit that without a victim, there can be no crime, your honour.

(And yes, I *know* I was a bit stroppy with the whole "I'm going to take the bus" thing. Mostly, I was embarrassed, and the girl I liked was looking at me like I'd just eaten a puppy or something. I didn't handle it well. But this does not mean that people—ahem, Ginny—should wind me up constantly about it. Every time I sound even the slightest bit cross, I immediately get a "Looks like Keith's getting on the bus again!" And it really must stop.)

There has been a great deal of debate recently about the level of truthfulness and honesty in books. Do you feel that *13 Little Blue Envelopes* is an accurate representation of events?

It seems fairly accurate, at least judging from the bits I was in. But I would also like to say that the story is told very much from Ginny's point of view. And in Ginny's point of view, I seem to snore and borrow money more than I realize. About my captivating performances and gorgeous eyes . . . I can't comment on that and will move swiftly along.

I can assure you, however, that I do not have a "musty smell." Someone took liberties there.

Do you wear anything under your kilt?

I will only say that I wear my kilt in the traditional style.

In a world without Starbucks, what global corporation would you immortalize in song?

How fortunate that you should ask this question! I have, this very day, completed work on the first draft of "Bank: An Opera of Greed." You see, what I've done there is just remove the actual name of any bank, because a bank's a bank, really. In doing so, I was able to create a tour de force about the corrupting nature of money. I am, of course, looking for sponsors who would like to corrupt me with some of their filthy loot. I accept all currencies, and no amount is too small or too large. Please form an orderly queue.